ONLY THE HEART KNOWS HOW TO FIND THEM

ALSO BY CHRISTOPHER DE VINCK

The Power of the Powerless

ONLY THE HEART KNOWS HOW TO FIND THEM

Precious Memories for a

Faithless Time

CHRISTOPHER DE VINCK

VIKING

VIKING
Published by the Penguin Group
Viking Penguin, a division of Penguin Books USA Inc.,
375 Hudson Street, New York, New York 10014, U.S.A.
Penguin Books Ltd, 27 Wrights Lane, London W8 5TZ, England
Penguin Books Australia Ltd, Ringwood, Victoria, Australia
Penguin Books Canada Ltd, 10 Alcorn Avenue, Suite 300,
Toronto, Ontario, Canada M4V 3B2
Penguin Books (N.Z.) Ltd, 182–190 Wairau Road, Auckland 10, New Zealand

Penguin Books Ltd, Registered Offices: Harmondsworth, Middlesex, England

First published in 1991 by Viking Penguin, a division of Penguin Books USA Inc.

1 3 5 7 9 10 8 6 4 2

Some of the essays in this book first appeared in *About Issues, The American Scholar, Catholic New York, Catholic Sentinel, The Evangelist, The New World,* and *The Wall Street Journal.*

Grateful acknowledgment is made for permission to reprint the following
copyrighted material:
"Cracker Jack" song by permission of Borden, Inc. Cracker Jack is a registered
trademark of Borden, Inc.
Excerpt from "Danse Russe" from *Collected Poems 1909–1939, Volume I* by William Carlos Williams. Copyright 1938 by New Directions Publishing Corporation.
Reprinted by permission of New Directions Publishing Corporation.
Excerpt from "Hermit Crab" from *House of Light* by Mary Oliver. Copyright ©
1990 by Mary Oliver. Reprinted by permission of Beacon Press.

LIBRARY OF CONGRESS CATALOGING IN PUBLICATION DATA
De Vinck, Christopher, 1951–
Only the heart knows how to find them : precious memories for a faithless time
/ Christopher de Vinck.
p.   cm.   ISBN 0-670-83876-4
1. De Vinck, Christopher, 1951–   —Family. 2. De Vinck family.
3. Catholics—United States—Biography. 4. Family—United States—
Philosophy.
I. Title.
CT275.D317A3   1991   973.92′0922—dc20   91-50142   [B]

Printed in the United States of America
Set in Bodoni Book
Designed by Jessica Shatan

To Roe

and to our children,

David, Karen, and Michael

FROM THE NORTH

Before we stepped into the summer cottage
My father and I leaned back upon the
Grass to guess the direction of the next
Falling star.

I do not know much about constellations
Or the fortunes hooked to each.

I do not know if God chose
To keep earth in one position.

That night, with all the world's weight
To our backs, and the arch of the universe
Above us, my father in that hidden season
And I stopped time between us.

"There, Chris! From the north!"

A flare and streak of light which I
Still keep in all that I am and in
All that I wish to teach my children
Before they sleep: "From the north."

I would like to thank the following people who were directly responsible for the creation of this book: Jim Brieg, Mary Claire Gart, Bob Pfohman, Barbara Phillips, Tim Ferguson, Jim Trelease, Rafe Sagalyn, and Mindy Werner.

CONTENTS

Preface   xv

1•Childhood   1

Father   5
Gathering the Flames of Spring   9
The Good Stuff   13
An Invitation   17
The Mystery in the Clay   21
Looking for a Shadow   25
Christmas Eve   31
The Balancing Act   39

2•Adolescence   43

A Man in the Crowd Waves Good-bye   47
The Chance to Live   49
Reflections on Light and Darkness   53
Rosie   57
How to Find Arcturus   61
Under the Brave Passage of Time   65

Contents

Illuminations   69
The Reunion   73

3•Marriage   77

First Love   81
Ladies and Gentlemen   85
Anniversary   89
Vows   93

4•Family   97

Buried Treasure   101
A Daughter's Question   105
Kissing the Toaster   109
In the Eye of the Storm   113
Fatherhood   119
A Father's Advice   123

5•Career   127

Pigeonholes   131
The Juggler   135
The Choice   139
Ignorance   143
A Morning's Attitude   147

Contents

Dreams of a Weary Commuter   149

Children Know Best   151

6•Loneliness   155

Acceptance   159

The Secrets We Keep   163

Simplicity, Simplicity, Simplicity   167

Adrift in a Moonlit Kayak   171

Gifts   175

A Perch Used to View the World   179

7•Looking Back   183

An Impulse Is Given   187

Swimming with the Sea Turtle   191

The Day the Elephant Tree Died   195

In the Beauty of Our Stillness   199

Autumn Boys and Acorn Pipes   203

The Bear   207

Through the Looking Glass   211

The Wind Machine   215

PREFACE

Willa Cather wrote, "Most of the basic material a writer works with is acquired before the age of fifteen."

I think the type of material she spoke about was the material of the heart: harmony and innocence discovered early on in our lives. Much of Huck Finn's adventures came from Mark Twain's early boyhood. Much of Harper Lee's novel *To Kill a Mockingbird* was born in those early days of her own life, before she was fifteen. But the experience is not enough. A notion, too, needs to be created, a sense for it all.

This book is a collection of memories, and in memory there stays with us the truth of our lives—not judicial truth, but poetic truth; not accurate evidence, but instead wisdom, that notion we spend the rest of our lives trying to recapture.

We do not live in a world of chaos, as this waning century seems to suggest, nor do we live in a world of constant joy. We live between the forces of doubt and faith. It is this clash of these invisible forces that attempts to destroy us and protect us at the same time. This is the struggle that defines our daily routine.

I do not see the power of the moon, nor do I see the power of the earth, but I do see the tide waters curl up from the distant sea and roll back and forth into nothingness. The blue water approaches the beach in beautiful foam, bubbling and roaring in a glorious display, but then it recedes, is finished, flat and silent. But the sea! It remains constant.

Memory is the sea, what is constant in our lives. It is there where we accumulate the habits of our own beauty or ugliness. The patterns of these habits are established before we are fifteen years old. It is in memory where we develop the notions that will sustain or destroy us.

From the home of my childhood I learned what a father was, what a mother was, what sisters and brothers were. I learned that the wind made an extraordinary whistling sound as it rushed past the weather stripping of the front door. It was from this house that I discovered the power of reading and the delight of a praying mantis sitting on the stone wall in August.

As we grow older we tend to focus our attentions upon

those things we trusted and believed in when we were children. We just have to know where to find them.

When I tell you that this book is about childhood and adolescence, about marriage and family; when I tell you this book is about careers and loneliness, I am really telling you this book is about the voices of my mother and father. I am trying to re-create the sounds of my brothers and sisters hooting and laughing in the woods beyond my vision, waiting for me to join them.

I am trying to tell you that to love our wives and husbands, to love our children, to do good work, to endure loneliness, we must have memories of what it was like to be loved, and those memories will always protect us.

From the home of my childhood I have brought nothing but
precious memories, for there are no memories more
precious than those of early childhood in one's first home.
And that is almost always so if there is any love and
harmony in the family at all. Indeed, precious memories
may remain even of a bad home, if only the heart knows
how to find what is precious.

The Brothers Karamazov

—FYODOR DOSTOYEVSKY

ONLY THE HEART KNOWS HOW TO FIND THEM

·1·

CHILDHOOD

When we were children

Spring was easy.

— LOUIS MACNEICE

FATHER

I first heard the voice when I was three or four years old as my father recited "Baa, Baa, Black Sheep." I do not remember if we were sitting on my bed, but I do remember his long arms around me, and I remember a large tree.

When I think about my father, I often remember swinging from the sugar maple that grew against our house. The extended branches. The bending leaves. I truly felt cradled, never fearing that the boughs would break. This is how I felt in my father's arms.

But I discovered a new security for the first time when he recited "Baa, baa, black sheep, have you any wooool. . . ." My father toyed and teased with the sound of a word as we all have done in our singsongs, on the chalked hopscotch boards, on the back-lot baseball grounds. The discovery of a new sound that pleases is the discovery of a new language, a universal language that is spoken in whispers each day. The trick is to be led to that sound, to be trained how to listen.

My father, like many fathers, anticipated the joy his child might feel at hearing a word stretched and pulled. He pressed his tongue against the roof of his mouth; pursed his lips in a tight, whistling position; forced a bit of extra air out of his lungs; and produced a wonderful sound: "wooool."

"Yes sir, yes sir, three bags fuuuull." Then it was time for bed.

The next time I heard the voice couldn't have been many years later.

When we were growing up, my parents took my brothers and sisters and me to Canada each July for two weeks. All of us children slept in a loft at the top of a small cabin my father built in 1960.

My parents often invited friends to visit us during this vacation. I remember an old Jesuit priest joined us for a few days. One evening, while we children were in a usual state of noise and fatigue, Father Gregory promised to tell us a story if we could hop into our pajamas, brush our teeth, and crawl under our blankets by the time he counted to a hundred.

"Ninety-eight. Ninety-nine. One hundred." And we were all in bed waiting to hear his story.

Father Gregory slowly climbed the little stairs my father made. When he reached the loft, he sat at the edge of one of the beds. I am sure it wasn't mine. Then, in the dark, he told us the story of Baba Yaga, a witch who lived in a house perched on chicken legs that ran around and around in the deep center of a forest somewhere in Russia.

I do not remember anything more about the story, but I will never forget Father Gregory's voice as it traveled over a greater distance than I could imagine when I was eight. Years later I read the works of the anthropologist Loren Eiseley, which helped me understand the magic of fresh darkness combined with a man's voice telling a story.

I believed and feared there was a Baba Yaga. I believed in her house tilting back and forth upon those terrible and thin yellow chicken legs, and I trusted the comfort and security of Father Gregory's voice.

As we grow older, we tend to focus our attentions upon those things we trusted and believed in when we were children. For me, it was that voice that had a familiar tone regardless of who spoke. In high school, one of my teachers read aloud Frank O'Connor's "Christmas Morning." In college, a professor read excerpts from *Billy Budd* and blew a bosun's whistle, and then I discovered the poets: Yeats, Williams, MacLeish. And I heard T. S. Eliot's recording of "The Love Song of J. Alfred Prufrock"—"Let us go then, you and I . . ."—and I realized that I had been there before, on my father's lap and in the darkness of a summer holiday.

There are many points of entry to that simple place we call beauty or comfort or security. For some of us it might have been the tune of a music box; for others a particular blush of color in the yard. For me it was that universal voice in the guise of good men telling stories, pulling and stretching words, blowing the bosun's whistle.

I believed in the voice of my father when I was a child. I believed in the stories, and rhymes again and again. Yes sir, yes sir, three bags full.

GATHERING THE
FLAMES OF
SPRING

One April long ago, before I reached an age when I ached for spring, my mother asked me to go into the yard and pick some daffodils for the dinner table. Such ideas seemed to be part of my daily life as a child: "Why don't you find some raspberries?" "Chrissy, let's go catch some lizards in the pond." "Why don't we try and sell lilacs?" "Anyone want to bake potatoes in the woods?"

"Do I need the clippers?"

"No, Chris. Just pull the flowers gently from the bottom of their stems."

I walked through the kitchen, held the leaf-embossed doorknob, pulled the door open, walked onto the porch, down the wood steps, and onto the grass. I liked the back yard.

Pine trees lined the left side, a wall of mountain laurel lined the right. I felt protected between the two walls of green. The grass was always thick and wild.

It is easy to be sidetracked from the task at hand. I was asked to gather daffodils, but already I was nearly lost among the smell of moist earth and the squirrel running tail up into the bush, annoyed that I interrupted his snack at the bird feeder.

Each time I looked in another direction there was something to admire: the maple tree in its new shades of green, ants running across the red and gray flagstones; Moses, my black cat, stretched like taffy upon the grass under the new sun.

It is easy to forget the responsibilities of a given task when we are surrounded with images of delight and beauty, each one a distraction.

"Chrissy, whatcha doin'?" someone, my sister Maria perhaps, called from an upstairs window.

"I'm getting flowers."

I walked down the steps of concrete and stone, past the serious iris plants, past the rose trellis, until I stood before the long, thin plot of fresh daffodils.

I leaned forward like Ferdinand the bull and s-m-e-l-l-e-d the flowers. Such hints of promise and hope.

I pulled one daffodil from the base of its stalk. I pulled another one, and another and another. Five. Ten. Twenty. A bundle for one hand, and then for the other. I picked them all!

"Christopher!" my mother called me from behind. I didn't realize that she had joined me in the garden.

"I'm finished. I got them all."

She began to laugh. I will always remember the laughter of my mother: full, loud, infectious, and easily sparked. Of course, at the time I didn't realize she was laughing with glee and puzzlement. She only wanted six or seven flowers for the dinner table. I would have picked all of Holland.

The daffodils began to ooze at the stems. My mother grabbed a bunch and held it at arm's length, and so I held my bunch at arm's length, and the two of us walked back toward the house carrying our flames of spring before us.

THE GOOD
STUFF

The house where I grew up sat on a hill. The green lawns and flower gardens sloped southward. At the bottom of the hill was where my father had guided a small stream into a pond he had built with sand and large stones.

To reach the pond my sisters and brothers and I had to run under the apple tree, which sagged like an old elephant, run past the sandbox, which my father had also built, run past the raspberry bushes to the right until we came to three small rock steps which led into the shallow water.

It is at this pond that I learned what the Halloween witches have known all along as they stir their black kettles under the light of the moon: deep inside the circle of water there is magic and spells and sudden mysteries.

Jewelweed, or what we called jewelweed, surrounded the pond. Its stem was green and tubular. In the spring it bloomed into small orange flowers. In the fall the seeds were wrapped in a thin, tight piece of vegetation which, when squeezed, exploded into your hand.

On my own one afternoon I discovered that the green leaves of the jewelweed turned into silver when I pressed them underwater.

I also discovered raccoon tracks pressed into the mud which surrounded the pond. I tried once to pour plaster into the prints to preserve their existence, but the plaster was too wet, so I buried the whole mess.

This is the pond where we children sailed four-inch plastic tugboats with clear marbles as the crew or treasure to be hauled across the open sea.

It was here that my sister Anne reached into the pond one afternoon to remove the stick that was submerged but pulled out instead a three-foot black snake with her bare hands. It was also here at this pond that we discovered the lizards.

Perhaps you believe paradise is like the Garden of Eden, or like some exotic weekend. I hope eternity has a place for a little boy in his brown shoes where he can stoop beside the clear water and look beyond his own image toward the silt and mud.

I can see myself there beside the water looking for lizards. These lizards were brown, about the length of your small finger, and about as thick as a shoelace. They had four legs, and two small dots for eyes.

Each of us has an activity from our past that we still remember doing.

I was Ahab pulling in the whale onto the deck of my four-inch plastic tugboat.

I was Houdini pulling magic out of the clear water.

I was a rotten brother chasing my little sister up the slope of the hill with a lizard in my closed fist, promising to send it down her back.

"Double, double toil and trouble; / Fire burn and cauldron bubble"—so said the witches of Shakespeare's *Macbeth*.

There was no better toil when I was eight than to sit beside my cauldron and stir my silver leaves into the water and return a dozen lizards to the mud and ooze.

The lizards are long gone, but my parents still live in their house upon the hill. By now the pond is dry, and the autumn leaves have hidden the depression in the earth.

Perhaps next spring, when the ground thaws and the stream flows again, there will be new life stirring at the bottom of my pond. I will not go there and hunt for lizards. That is the work of little boys and witches. Most adults just don't seem to be concerned about the good stuff squirming at the bottom of the waters.

AN INVITATION

Johnny and I were walking along the side of the road which overlooked the wide marsh to our right: bulrush, swamp, blackbirds, wild roses, and geese.

We were returning home from one of our many trips to town, perhaps with comic books under our arms and fresh gum in our mouths.

"Chris, what's that?" Johnny asked as he pointed toward a specific spot in the vast open space beyond our reach. At first I thought it was a goose swimming in the distance.

"I think it's a snake," Johnny said with conviction and with a sudden invitation: "Come on!"

I stood above him as he quickly ran down the embankment toward the marsh. I can still see his arms bouncing up and down in response to his running and jumping. He stood at the bottom of the hill waving and calling up, "Come on, Chrissy!"

I looked beyond Johnny and saw a thin question mark parting the water. I didn't think a snake could pull its body that high out of the marsh.

My first step down the hill pressed a stone into my shoe.

"Come on, Chrissy! It'll get away!"

I didn't know what Johnny intended to do with the snake. As I sat upon the ground to pull the stone from under my foot, Johnny began to run again.

By the time I reached him he was squatting at the edge of the marsh poking the water with a long stick.

"It got away."

In the cold months of winter Johnny and I spent many hours upon the frozen water of the marsh skating back and forth, chasing our sisters, polishing the ice with our mittens, and peering through the frozen water, looking nearly eye to eye with the large fish which passed under us like wandering spirits.

One spring we built a raft from old boards and chicken wire; it sank three feet from the shore.

When I was a sophomore in college, visiting home for the weekend, the phone rang. A reporter from the local newspaper asked, "Could you tell us a little about your neighbor Johnny

Lukaszewski?" Of course I didn't know what that meant coming from a reporter.

"Excuse me?"

"Your neighbor was killed in a car accident on the highway. A tractor trailer jumped the median and hit him head on. What would you like to say about him?"

I hung up.

I think about Johnny often. Would he too have three children by now? Would we still be friends?

I believe we are given hints of a true existence each day. I believe those hints extend beyond our habits of being and point toward a simple and clear eternity.

I believe a portion of heaven contains a wide, open marsh with geese, wild roses, blackbirds, and royal fish squinting up through the waters. I believe a boy is running ahead of me there, waving his arms up and down and calling out, "Come on, Chrissy!"

THE MYSTERY IN
THE CLAY

I understand the ancient carved heads tilting on Easter Island.
I understand the mysterious cave paintings sketched upon
the back walls of Lascaux. We human beings have a primary
agitation deep within us. We stir and twist inside the womb.
We grope toward the world of life, and in this life we try to
arrange the things around us in our own personal acts of
creation.

I tend to agree with William Butler Yeats, calling life a
spiral, a twisting down closer to the center around and around
in smaller and smaller circles. Some people think of life as
a single line: beginning to end. Some people think in terms
of a circle: all returns to itself eventually.

One afternoon when I was six, if there was a time when I

was six, my sister Anne and I discovered that there was a four-foot space under the back porch.

My grandfather had, the summer before, surrounded the base of the porch with walls of cemented rock which created a dark cave. My sister and I discovered the only entrance to this cave was through the basement window.

When the adults were occupied with writing or with company, Anne and I dragged an old carpet under the porch. We ran an extension cord along the basement beams and into our hideout, where we connected an old table lamp.

We were set: a carpet, a light. We brought in the Monopoly game, forbidden comic books, and the clay balls.

Deep within the woods of my father's land there was a monstrous oak tree that crashed during a heavy wind, pulling up its roots. At the base of the upturned roots, a small pool of water collected, and over the months a soft clay gathered at the bottom of this pool.

I remember how we scooped out the clay, rolled the moisture out, worked the dark earth into our hands until the clay was formed into a perfect sphere about the size of a tennis ball.

Anne and I made fourteen of these shapes. We let them dry in the sun. After a few days the clay hardened into a stiff grayness.

We carried these balls into the house when no one was looking. We crept down the basement stairs, opened the forbidden window, crawled up upon our bellies into the darkness, flicked the lamp on, and placed our fourteen balls into the far left-hand corner.

"Let's read some comic books."

"Yeah."

Whether it was on that particular day or during some other time, I do not remember; however, I do remember the look my grandmother had as she popped her head into our cave: a cross between Charles Dickens's Miss Pross defending England and a hornet.

"What are you children doing in this filth? Your mother is upstairs! Come right out!"

Well, my mother didn't wish to upset my grandmother, so Anne and I were forbidden to return to the cave, and my grandfather nailed the window shut.

That summer Anne and I built a terrific hut on the side lawn from bent mock-orange sticks and cut grass.

I believe, after thirty-two years, the carpet is still under the porch. I believe those fourteen clay balls are still in the far corner to the left. I do not look upon those things as a return to the beginning. Now that I think back to my childhood, I see more and more that I have been pushed over the side of nothingness and into the open, free currents of being. The spiral began. Children spun around and around a single afternoon, dodging a grandmother, stirring the clay in the waters.

I now seek the continued creation of my poetry. I seek the continued creation of my three children's freedom. I seek the continued creation of my marriage with Roe.

In the play *Man of La Mancha* Don Quixote said on his deathbed, "I just wanted to add a measure of grace to the world."

Children do not understand that their play is the first turn of that creation. We human beings are destined to create life from nothingness. Artists know this; mothers and fathers know this; writers know this.

To reject the mystery of mixing clay and water into a visible shape, to reject the power of crawling upon our bellies into the darkness with a magic secret, is to reject the distinction between the beauty which is human, and the beast which is lost in nothingness.

LOOKING FOR A
SHADOW

This year my son David wishes to be Robin Hood. My daughter, Karen, would like to be a witch, and Michael, my youngest child, will be a skeleton. The season has turned away from August heat, and the pumpkin my children and I picked from the vegetable stand is already carved and grinning on the front steps.

I suppose Halloween belongs to children, all those chocolate bars and doorbells, but I cannot help feeling a little jealous on this night of prowling spirits. Somewhere among the dry leaves and voices echoing throughout the neighborhood, somewhere between the rattling cornstalks and melting candles, I too look for my own long shadow cast out across the lawns and sidewalks.

More than Christmas and birthdays, more than the Fourth of July, Halloween reminds me how far I've come from all that was pure and simple.

The face that I shave each morning becomes more and more the face of my father and grandfather. I wear a jacket and tie to work. I know my Social Security number by heart. I've been tested by ETS, polled by the GOP, charted by actuarial studies, granted a B.A., an M.A., and an Ed.D. I have credit-card numbers, a driver's-license number, checking accounts, savings accounts. My house is number 11. It is difficult to escape the masks which the world seems to adjust upon our faces.

When I was young and it was spring and daffodils, and the world was the distant cry of a catbird or the voice of Johnny calling from across the street for a game of ball, I'd often run to the woods behind my father's house to the fallen oak tree, where the clay waited for me. I'd press my fingers deep into the mud, and draw two lines on either side of my face. It had something to do with pirates and Indians and robbers, but now I think it was more my desire to mingle with the earth, to become part of all that was growing. We change best when we are hidden. Moths know this, as do lovers and children. I did not understand this the year I discovered what I thought to be the best Halloween costume.

In the middle of October when I was twelve, I found in the attic, deep inside a metal trunk, a tuxedo with tails, a pleated shirt, pants with velvet stripes running down both sides, and a bow tie. After quickly taking off my clothes, my blue jeans and T-shirt, I slowly dressed in the clothes my father had abandoned when he left the ballrooms of Belgium and his youth to come to America in 1948.

I slipped the last button into the hole and tucked the shirt into the pants, ran downstairs in my bare feet to my brother's room, where I found the bowler hat he had brought home from London one year. I ran to my mother's room and scratched a small mustache onto my upper lip with eyeliner. I found a cane in my grandmother's closet; then I ran to the living room and waddled before my father and mother like the Charlie Chaplin I was so sure to be on the streets of Halloween in 1963.

"Take them off," was all my father said. "Please take them off and put them back where you found them, the clothes."

I didn't know then my father too had shadows of himself kept hidden inside old trunks and memories.

That Halloween I was a hobo.

So it is now with ambivalence that each new Halloween I greet, again, the children who come to my door dressed in hunchbacks and crooked teeth, witch hats, and angel wings. They always seem to know the night is theirs; they also seem to know they will soon be able to wash off the makeup and peel off the latex masks and return to themselves whole, intact.

I watch the younger children arrive at my door first, with their mothers or fathers waiting in the background at the end of the walk. Then the older children, in packs of six or eight, come and hoot and laugh as I drop a Hershey Bar into each of their open pillowcases. "Thank you," they say in singsong one by one.

But soon it will be nine o'clock, perhaps nine-thirty, and the last children will come: two older boys usually, embarrassed because they feel beyond the age of trick-or-treating. They will have wrinkled shopping bags in their hands, plastic cigars in their mouths, or rumpled hats on their heads, simply to justify their ringing my doorbell.

Each year I wait for these boys. I empty all the remaining candy I have into their bags. They laugh at their good fortune, thank me, sling their sacks over their shoulders, turn, and walk down the steps in silence. I watch their long legs carry them across the grass. I watch them walk down the road as the streetlamp casts their shadows out before them. I always have the impulse to shout, "Wait for me," as I stretch my neck out my front door and watch them slowly walk beyond the yellow light and step into the darkness. Do they know they have lost a part of themselves, these older boys?

The Celts thought long ago that the cold air of Halloween brought home the ghosts and spirits of deceased relatives from barren fields. I think of scarecrows and witches, specters and apparitions stepping slowly among the pumpkins and dried cornstalks. I can nearly see these spirits walking back through a moonless autumn night to look at the homes and into the windows of their living children and grandchildren.

We the living wear upon our faces the masks, hints, and shadows of our grandparents and great-grandparents. The center DOES hold, from generation to generation. The Celts probably knew this. Despite the decay and cold, they lit fires and wore masks to trick the night away. We hold, still, within ourselves a purity of heart. Let us take a lesson from the children and carry our good fortune with us in the dark, from streetlight to streetlight.

CHRISTMAS
EVE

Anne could endure a Monopoly game longer than anyone on the block, so it was her suggestion to gather up popcorn, Christmas cookies, apple juice, and the Monopoly game and head up to her room, where we could keep the radio low and listen to the continuous Christmas music, and where she could ruin me with her great skill and finesse, I thought, by acquiring Boardwalk, Park Place, and all the green, orange, yellow, and red sets, and every hotel that wasn't lost under the piano or in the sandbox. It was our plan to stay up until midnight so we could open our stockings.

It was a tradition in our house that we could open our Christmas stockings at midnight of Christmas Eve, because, my father reasoned, by then it really was Christmas. Anne and I believed in the magic of that fancy rule because it was the only night of the year when we could stay up for as long as we wished.

Well before eleven o'clock our parents were in bed. My little brother and sister were in bed. My older brother took the station wagon to his girl friend's house. He was going to midnight mass, which gave Anne and me an even greater incentive to stay up: "If he can do it, so can we." His being out also gave us a sense of maturity, of holding down the fort, waiting for his late-night return.

The house where I grew up was built in 1900, clad in cedar shingles, lined with oak floors, and heated by a converted coal-burning furnace which looked like a bathyscaph. For years I refused to step into the basement by myself in fear that at any moment the furnace would, behind my back, start up and swallow me. When the furnace clicked on, we heard this great roar throughout the house.

Because the house was heated with steam, we were entertained all winter by a copper-and-water ensemble: radiators clanking, hissing, and popping. I thought it was wonderful. And because the house was so old, there was no such thing as zone heating or climate control, which meant that the house was heated unevenly. The living room was pleasant, the kitchen always warm. The front hall, where the telephone was kept, was cold enough to preserve our fresh fruits and vegetables. Anne's bedroom was always so hot only Dante and an armadillo could fully appreciate it.

I rolled the dice and landed on Pennsylvania, which belonged to Anne, and which had a red hotel. I didn't have enough cash, only a few gold hundred-dollar bills, and a sloppy pile of pink fives and white singles. I couldn't pay my fine. I began to plead for mercy, and sniffle a bit, so Anne began to make deals. She wanted all my railroads and my Get Out of Jail Free card, *and* the last cookie I had been saving.

I licked the cookie right away and was about to make her a counteroffer of two railroad cards when she said something about the heat in the room, then stood up.

Most of the windows in our house that opened didn't have storm windows, so it was not difficult for cold air to pass quickly into the bedroom. Anne opened the window about an inch, which was just enough.

I was staring at the Monopoly board, nearly falling asleep, when Anne asked me to turn the radio off and come to the window. We both knelt on the floor; our chins rested on the windowsill. Then Anne said, "Listen."

We are taught in school to hear things in a poem. We are taught to pay attention, told to look closely, instructed to underline and take notes, but because of the way Anne said, "Listen," in a whisper, in a slight question, I knew something was really up. We listened together.

Our neighborhood had clear divisions. We never knew the people across the street because they didn't have children and because the street was a busy turnpike which we were forbidden to cross. The family to our right had dogs and two older boys. The family to the left were our best friends. And there was the nursing home.

I knew two things about old people when I was ten: my grandmother and the nursing home across the street. My grandmother was open, alone, full of stories and complaints. The nursing home was dark, set off from the road, and quiet. I often saw a wheelchair on the front porch, or two fragile women in thick-heeled shoes walking arm in arm back and forth along the drive.

"Go shut the lights," Anne whispered.

Somehow we are able to hear things better in the darkness. As I closed the lights and rejoined Anne at the windowsill, I tripped over the Monopoly board, which ended the game.

We knelt at the window and heard over the distance of brown lawns and black night a slow, faint chorus singing "Joy to the world . . ." accompanied by rigid piano playing. And we listened and listened and listened.

"Let's go see them," Anne suggested. To me the idea of going out of the house in the middle of the night without a grownup was like asking me to sleep in the basement with the furnace. It just wasn't done. But we went anyway.

As we left Anne's bedroom, I was surprised to see that the

rest of the house was dark, except for the front-porch light waiting for my brother's return. The vague silhouette of the Christmas tree in the living room, the yellow porch light, the cold floors all suggested a dream. We have all walked along this light, especially when we are in pain or afraid. I was afraid.

"I just want to see them sing," Anne reassured me as we buttoned our coats and pulled on our wool hats and mismatched gloves.

We left the house just as it was: the tree, the family sleeping, the one porch light. I let Anne hold my hand. We could hear the driveway stones crunch under our feet. The air kissed our cheeks with little affection. The stars were up and bright, and the singing from the nursing home was just a bit louder. "Hark! the herald angels sing, / Glory to the newborn King. Peace on earth . . ."

It was easy enough to cross the forbidden street, because there weren't any cars. I was half hoping my brother would appear in the station wagon and drag us home to safety.

I was afraid. We were trespassing; I didn't know the word existed when I was ten, but I knew the feeling, and when we turned to look at our house it looked crooked or backward. I had never seen it from this direction before.

"Peace on earth and mercy mild, / God and sinners reconciled . . ."

I suggested we turn back; Anne suggested we walk to the

side of the nursing home and look in the wide picture window. She won.

The house looked like a jack-o'-lantern; the singing was uneven and low. Then I remembered how each night my grandmother would leave the bathroom at the end of the hall with a glass holding water and her false teeth rinsing inside. So I matched everything I knew about old people with all my fears of the dark, of getting in trouble, of witches living in huts supported by chicken legs, and then we turned the corner and looked deep inside the nursing home.

It was a large room, probably the reception room, or the all-purpose room. There were four or five poinsettias with gold paper wrapped around the pots sitting on the floor, and two or three on the table. There was a Christmas tree with two or three strings of lights that blinked, and, sitting in a horseshoe pattern, each on a metal folding chair, thirty or forty old, old men and women were gathered around a piano player who was just as old as all the rest.

Anne and I stood outside, framed in the window, watching. No one noticed us.

How can I describe the expression we saw on their faces? Not stunned, but still. Not puzzled, but searching. I can only describe what I saw with today's memory. At ten years old I probably thought they were dead. It is enough to say that what I saw through the window was one of the first glimpses

I ever had of those incongruent possibilities. "Why aren't they home? It's Christmas!" I blurted out.

Anne quickly slapped her hand over my mouth at the same time that a woman, the one with a red-and-green ribbon in her hair, turned and saw us: our crooked hats, our mismatched gloves, our wide eyes. I nearly bit Anne's finger.

Then this woman's empty face turned simply into a smile and she nodded her head up and down just a bit.

Anne—stupidly, I thought at the time—waved too, then I waved, then the old woman waved back, and the world seemed to stop.

One by one the other people noticed that our new friend was waving, so they began to turn toward the window, but it was too late. Anne and I had already started running.

"Silent night, Holy night. / All is calm, all is bright. . . ." We ran and we ran, across the street, against the gray crunching stones of our driveway, up the porch steps, and back into our house; then we slowly closed the door behind us.

"Do you think they'll tell?" I asked in a panic. "Are we going to get in trouble? I liked the one with the ribbon in her hair! Why did you cover my mouth? I couldn't breathe!"

"Shhh. It's Christmas," Anne whispered. "It's past midnight. We can open our stockings now."

That had a calming effect.

We turned on one lamp in the living room and walked to

the fireplace, where our stockings were hanging from the mantel. Anne's was the green one with pearls and bells sewn along the edges; mine was the one made from a cloth of printed clowns and circus dogs.

Anne unwrapped one of those nesting Russian wooden dolls and a tea set that fit in a matchbox. I found in my stocking a bag of chocolate coins, a magnifying glass, and a magic trick where you could make a small ball appear and disappear. We both received red, green, and yellow marzipan candies in the shape of little fruit.

"Let's go," Anne whispered. We jumped up. I quickly popped a marzipan strawberry into my mouth; then we ran upstairs.

At her bedroom door Anne whispered again, saying, "Don't tell Mom"; then she kissed me, but I survived.

I ran to my room, where my little brother slept, took off my clothes, and crawled into bed. I heard my older brother enter the house and lock the back door. He turned off the light, and walked to his room.

I have read Dylan Thomas and *Faustus*, I watched Ebenezer Scrooge's door knocker change into Marley's ghost, but I have never felt as much the combination of joy and sadness and mystery as I felt on that Christmas Eve of so long ago.

THE BALANCING
ACT

Between the garage and the chicken coop of my father's house there was a tall green fence. My sisters and brothers knew how to climb up that fence, balance themselves there, and walk along the very edge from one end to the other.

I still see my sister . . . arms stretched out on either side of her. Those were the years when I could not piece together the images that were placed before me. The cherry tree bloomed in feather balls each spring. The skunk cabbage grew into green elephant ears. I knew the names of the birds— robins, woodcock, thrush—but I didn't know why. These things were part of the drama, props for the neighborhood.

Who knew to look at the world, really look at the world for clues to some distant beauty?

One afternoon I stepped up to the fence alone. I reached with both arms above my head and grabbed the top. I pressed my right foot upon the fence the way I had seen my brother do and began slowly pulling myself up. The wood cut into my hands. My arms began to ache. Eventually I swung one leg over the top of the fence and sat there upon the edge. There was a small ledge, the brace of wood along the entire length of the fence which kept the pieces in place and which made for a place where I could stand. I was alone. I slowly walked along the top from one side to the other until I lunged out and grabbed the roof of the chicken coop. I made it.

I have dared to climb the fence many times since then: the first time I gave a speech before five hundred people in Chicago, the time I resigned from a job because of a great ugliness. We are all asked to do things that take courage, and we human beings have an extraordinary capacity to believe that, indeed, things can get done.

We can look around us and see clearly how easy it is to be knocked off balance and fall from the ledge of our existence. But something keeps us standing erect, an invisible force, a choice to live, a hope, a faith in the journey and in the journey's end.

All is not forgotten in the eyes of God or in the heart of a faithful man or woman. See the green fence? Remember the approach? The ascent? The journey across? Hook your sorrows and joys to the invisible umbrella in your hand, keeping you balanced. Dance across the narrow edge of the universe, which has been given to you alone to recognize, accept, and conquer.

·2·

ADOLESCENCE

The parasol girls slept,

sun-sitting their

lovely years.

—ANNE SEXTON

A MAN IN THE
CROWD WAVES
GOOD-BYE

When I was a teenager, and the greatest distance for me was the next town, beyond a small lake, I was sitting on the living-room couch looking through one of the family photo albums. They were pictures my father took when he was a young man: my mother leaning against a tree, great-aunts in dark dresses, my older brother in shorts holding a model of a toy car.

I continued casually to turn each page of the album, trying to match the images on my lap with the sound of my mother typing upstairs or with the appearance of my father, who was approaching me. He stopped, leaned over my shoulder, and didn't speak.

I turned one page, and then another; suddenly my father

said with a slight hesitation in his voice, "You see that picture, Christopher?"

"Yes."

"What do you see?"

"Well, I see water, and in the distance many buildings."

"Look closely beyond the fence."

"I can see people. They look very small."

I can tell you now that the photograph was taken from a
departing ship, the photographer taking a picture of the distant Belgian port decreasing in size. My father asked me to
look closely at one particular figure.

"The man with his one arm raised above his head?"

"Yes. That is my father waving good-bye to your mother
and me as we sailed for America. It is the last time I ever
saw him."

My father stepped into the kitchen, or out to the yard. I
looked and looked at the small outline of a man in the photograph leaning against a tall chain-link fence as he waved
and waved and waved.

You can build an entire civilization on a single idea or
philosophy. I believe you can build an entire existence upon
a single gesture passed along from person to person, a con-
nection made across the deep waters, beyond time, held in
a still photograph for a teenager to see and, ultimately, to
understand.

THE CHANCE
TO LIVE

"The German troops were advancing into Belgium. We could hear explosions. I was so frightened. 'My arms,' I said to your grandmother. 'My arms! I am afraid that they will shoot off my arms.' "

My mother was a teenager in May 1940, and because she was so frightened, she and my grandmother fled their Brussels home, crossed over the French border, and became refugees. They didn't know where they were going except far away from the bombs.

After much travel, after much exhaustion, they arrived in a small town on the coast of France: Dunkirk.

"There were so many people. Families like us carrying suitcases, children crying, planes flying overhead. And the soldiers. There were thousands and thousands of soldiers. We simply thought this was normal, probably what the rest of the world was experiencing at the moment. We didn't know at the time that the British troops were pushed to the sea and were stranded, waiting for any possible help their country might, and did, send across the channel to rescue them.

"But we were not troops. We were three hungry, tired people in search of a hotel."

Of course my family couldn't find a hotel, and it became obvious to my grandmother that they had to leave this city of turmoil. They walked to the bus station, where there were hundreds of people waiting for one of the last buses to leave Dunkirk.

"We were in the front of the mob. We waited and waited. In the distance we saw the bus making its way through the mass of people."

Have you ever been in a crowd when suddenly the people from the rear begin to move forward like a wave and all who are in the front are shoved?

"When the crowd saw the bus," my mother told me, "everyone began to push. The bus approached closer and closer and the crowd increased its fury. Closer and closer the bus arrived. I could see the driver. The doors began to pass us, the front wheels. Then the crowd gave a sudden heave and I was thrown under the bus. I can still see the road coming up to my face and the large rear wheels rolling toward me."

My grandmother saw my mother being thrown under the bus, and she screamed and screamed at the driver to stop.

Above the roar of the crowd the driver managed to hear my grandmother and he stopped the bus.

He stepped out and asked my grandmother what the trouble was.

"My daughter. She has been pushed under the bus!"

The driver and my grandmother stooped under the crowd, and there was my mother, flat on her back, with the rear wheels of the bus rolled upon the side of her outstretched dress.

"The bus was so surrounded with people that the driver couldn't back it up. My dress had to be cut so that I could crawl out.

"Then the driver turned to your grandmother and said, 'Because your daughter had such a fright, your family may have the first seat on the bus.' "

My mother and my grandmother climbed in. The crowd pressed forward, filling the remaining seats quickly, and the bus drove off, leaving most of the other people behind.

So much would have been lost in the history of my family had the wheels rolled six inches more: my brothers and sisters, my own life . . . my children, David, Michael, and Karen.

Our lives are held together by a thin thread of circumstance.

REFLECTIONS ON
LIGHT AND
DARKNESS

One of the saddest moments in the day is when the sunlight can still be seen against the highest leaves of the maple trees, something like a crown of flames above the slowly graying woods below. Throughout the spring and summer a single robin creates an evening song to the dying of this light. The robin's song at dusk is the second-most-poignant sound I have ever heard. The first is the painfully beautiful music of Aaron Copland.

I do not understand much about the creation of light. My brother-in-law, a scientist, tried to explain it to me once, something about waves and electrons. But all that he said doesn't seem to match what I see at night sometimes when I go to bed.

Some years ago Roe and I were able to arrange the construction of an addition to our two-bedroom home. At the time our three children were sleeping in a single room.

During the renovations we had to remove the bathroom window. "Perhaps," Roe suggested, "we could add a skylight to the bathroom? It's so dark in there now." So a skylight was added.

It is a wonderful thing to walk up the dark staircase at midnight and step into the bathroom. Often there is a perfect rectangle of bluish light against the bathroom floor. It is the moon's light traveling over a distance of 239,000 miles for my convenience and delight.

We like our Fourth of July fireworks, the yellow flames of a campfire reflecting against our cheeks, fireflies blinking in the hot August night.

One summer evening in 1968, during our vacation, my father and I leaned back against the side of the station wagon and tried to see if we could notice any communication satellites passing overhead in the Canadian sky. We could. A single spot of light moved across the blackness.

I like to think how every human being has been touched by the sun's light. I like to think about the hall light my mother always left on in the house where I grew up.

It is said that before the atom bomb explodes to its full fury there is a frightful blinding white light that flashes about all that exists, a gathering up of all color and life into a single element easily crushed in a single explosion.

I just finished reading Ernst Schnabel's essay "A Tragedy Revealed: A Heroine's Last Days," a *Life*-magazine essay about Anne Frank printed in 1958. "She, too, still had her face, up to the very last. To the last also she was moved by the dreadful things the rest of us had somehow become hardened to. Who bothered to look when the flames shot up into the sky at night from the crematoriums? Who was troubled that every day new people were being selected and gassed? Most of us were beyond feeling. But not Anne. I can still see her standing at the door and looking down the camp street as a group of naked gypsy girls were driven by on their way to the crematorium. Anne watched them going and cried. And she also cried when we marched past the Hungarian children who had been waiting half a day in the rain in front of the gas chambers."

All the forces of evil work at the creation of darkness. We need to teach our young people to look for the light against the maple trees at dusk and to celebrate the blue moon, but we also need to teach them to remember the light of the terrible flames which shot up into the night's sky.

ROSIE

I still believed as a teenager that deep inside the forests of Russia Baba Yaga the witch lived in her house supported by two chicken legs.

Psychologists have determined that fairy tales are part of our collective subconscious, little stories we carry with us which bounce around inside us, perhaps trying to rearrange all that is neat and orderly in our lives.

What is created for the imagination gives power and delight to what exists in our real world.

I would not have been surprised if Rosie's house had sprouted chicken legs. Rosie was, I thought, like Glinda in *The Wizard of Oz*, a good witch, the good witch from Mallison Street. She was our babysitter for many, many years when I was a child, and she never took any money for all the times she spent with my brothers and sisters and me.

Rosie's husband died young. Her oldest son died of cancer. Her granddaughter died of cancer. Her youngest son has bravely combated cancer all his life. When Rosie was in her early twenties, one of her breasts was removed.

On Friday afternoons we could see from a distance Rosie walking up the street in her long coat and kerchief in the winter, or in her light, checkered dress in the summer. She always carried a cloth bag which produced crayons, coloring books, connect-the-dots books, and candy.

It was as if we could say, "Boil little pot, boil," and all the joy of a holiday would spill over the top of Rosie's cloth bag and into our laps.

About once a month my brothers and sisters and I would be invited to spend the evening at Rosie's house. Her kitchen was lit for the night with a small, single bulb which gave the room a soft, inside-of-a-pumpkin glow. In the bottom right-hand drawer of her cabinet Rosie had every type of candy: Three Musketeers, Milky Ways, Turkish Taffy, M & M's. I would not have been surprised if the roof and shingles of Rosie's house had been made of gingerbread.

In her sunroom she had shelf upon shelf of African violets: purple ones, pink ones, blue ones. "They like tea," Rosie said as she poured small drops of brown liquid into each plant. The very idea of serving tea to a population of African violets gave much credence to Alice's wild party with the mad March Hare in Wonderland.

Rosie liked to sit in her side porch and have you sit beside her. She liked to talk about New York City and what it was like when she was a girl: the parrot the trolley conductor kept on his shoulder, the sinking of a ferryboat which killed many church-picnic goers and how she couldn't go that morning because she had diphtheria. Rosie liked to talk about the convict she had helped, about gathering horse manure for the garden, about her famous bridge games over at the firehouse. Her stories were just as good as the *Arabian Nights*.

There are perhaps fifty people who even knew that Rosie ever existed. Perhaps you have a Rosie down your street, across from you in your building, or deep in your memory.

As I grew older, and the need for a babysitter ended, I still returned to Rosie's house to sit beside her. She threw out all the flowers. "Too much work," she said. Her candy drawer was empty. She installed fluorescent lights in her kitchen, but one of the last times we were together in her house (which might have swayed back and forth just a bit) Rosie led me into her dining room to her glass-and-wood hutch.

On the top shelf sat a small wooden figure: a smiling Buddha from Korea. He sat there, round and fat, with painted black hair, a red shirt, and gold buttons.

"If you put a nickel on his head, you'll get some money

in a week." She explained how a month before she had tried her luck and within a few days a child threw his mother's purse out the car window. When Rosie found and returned it, the woman gave her ten dollars.

I dug into my pocket for the feel of a thick gray coin, and then I placed it upon the Buddha's head.

I never knew what happened to the doll or to my nickel. Rosie became ill, sold her house, moved to a nursing home, and died, but I can tell my children that "Once upon a time there was an old woman who lived in a house. And deep inside that house there were flowers and candy, a soft light, and a smiling Buddha."

I owe much of my imagination to Rosie, because she was nearly too good to be real.

HOW TO FIND
ARCTURUS

The boys are in the tent: David and two of his neighborhood friends. They decided that the tent ought to face the west, that they would sleep with the flaps down and with one flashlight pointing toward the ceiling.

It is ten-fifteen in the evening and I can still hear them talking and laughing as I write.

We human beings like to place things in the wilderness: our carved initials in a tree, a birdbath, a cabin, ourselves.

I lived in a dorm during my first year at the university. It was a difficult year for me: leaving home, living with people I did not trust or admire, taking notes in philosophy class about beauty and virtue, then returning to the dorms, where drugs, beer, and basketball took precedent over Aristotle, Kant, and Socrates.

By the end of October in my freshman year I had seen enough. The drinking, the swearing, the drugs. I went to bed with my clothes on, and waited until my two roommates were asleep. At two in the morning I slipped out of my bed, stepped out into the dimly lit hallway, walked down four flights of stairs and into the cool night air of the courtyard. I was going home. Four hundred miles. I could walk that.

At the front of the school was a large expanse of grass and fields which led in the direction of the town. That is where I headed.

I will never forget that night. As I began to walk through the open field, I noticed the night's stillness, and the stars.

"If you follow down with your finger the three stars of the Big Dipper's handle," I could nearly hear my astronomy professor explaining, "and if you continue to trace toward the left in the night sky, you will come upon the star Arcturus."

I found the Big Dipper, or it found me, and, sure enough, I also found Arcturus, neatly labeled in my mind.

The dim lights of the university were to my back. The buildings were dark except for a rectangle of light here and there like the sneer of a jack-o'-lantern.

During those first two months I smelled marijuana for the first time, I saw a *Playboy* magazine for the first time, saw a classmate so drunk that he staggered down the hallway slashing a bayonet against the walls just before he threw up and passed out into his own filth.

One of the last things my father had said to me before I stepped onto the bus for my first trip to the university was "Don't let college interfere with your education."

Good advice, I thought as I headed due east in the middle of the night in the middle of my youth, heading out, walking home, quitting college.

The well-trimmed grass eventually turned into coarse, cut hay, and the field narrowed toward the edge of the woods. I saw the stars, I felt my heavy coat upon my shoulders, I heard my shoes press against the dryness under my feet. That is when I noticed a dark, slow movement in the tall brush at the very lip of the trees and bramble.

At first I thought it was just a false vision, or the wind pushing against the low leaves and branches, but then through the blue darkness I saw a blanket and a young man and woman asleep in their embrace.

Soon after, I turned around and walked back to the dorm, undressed, and went to bed.

I transferred out of that school the following year, completed college, married, taught, wrote, gave myself over to poetry, to Roe, and to the children.

The clearest image that stays with me from my first two years of college, the image that seemed right among all that seemed wrong, was the vision of youth under the blanket away from the buildings, lectures, and contradictions, that vision of youth embracing under the bold night stars.

I should have taught the boys in the yard tonight how to find Arcturus, but now it is midnight, they are asleep, and, besides, it is something they must discover on their own.

UNDER THE BRAVE
PASSAGE OF
TIME

I have always admired the moon. When I was a child I kept the empty toilet-paper roll and used it as a telescope when the moon was full or half full. I kept notes in my used school pads on the shape of the moon, the clouds that passed before the face, the distance between the moon's body and my own bedroom window, which I calculated to be about three miles. I believed "Good Night Moon" by Margaret Wise Brown was written for me, that there really was a man in the moon, and I wished cows could jump that high.

In the summer of 1969 I was seventeen years old. One evening I was swimming in a blue pool with Jack and Harry and Ellen. The four of us dared each other to leap from the rock, over the concrete and stones, and dive into the distant water. We took turns: back dives, flips, shallow dives, cannonballs, belly flops accompanied by much laughter. The real idea was to impress Ellen.

We swam around her, dove under the clear water to admire her legs or to sneak up behind her and snap the elastic band upon her back which kept her bathing suit in place.

As the night air dropped in temperature, we all stepped out of the pool. Our skin rippled with goose bumps as we quickly dried our bodies with wide, sail-like towels, Jack, Harry, Ellen, and I.

The four of us stepped down into the woods toward Ellen's house. I do not remember what we spoke about. Perhaps we didn't speak.

The moon is one of the saddest objects in the sky, for it goes through much pain as it changes shape, endures a passive position at the mercy of the brave sun. Teenagers bear much of the same pain, this constant change in the finite circle of themselves, which they cannot control under the brave passage of time that is against them, though they do not believe it is so, or swim in the night to deny it is so.

As the four of us entered Ellen's house, her parents called us into the living room.

"You're just in time. They are about to land on the moon."

I vaguely knew the space agency had sent up some astronauts and they were going to try for the first moon landing of a human being. At the time I was more interested in Ellen than in history.

I watched with the rest of the nation as Neil Armstrong placed his foot upon the dry surface of the moon while his voice echoed in our consciousness: "That's one small step for a man, one giant leap for mankind."

I have on my wall a whimsical sculpture by Carruth. I do not know who Carruth is, but I like what the artist created: a king playing a flute to a cat, a fish, and the crescent moon. They all seem to be smiling. Perhaps the music is sweet. Perhaps the darkness inspires whimsy.

Jack and Ellen eventually married. He became a fine lawyer, and she a physical therapist. They have three children.

Tonight out my window as I write there is a full moon. I look up with pleasure at the silver disk in silken mist and feel like playing a flute.

I do not wish to believe there are footprints on the moon's surface; I prefer still to believe that my toilet-paper telescope revealed all that we human beings need to see there: whimsy, the sorrows of a changing face, Ellen swimming back and forth under the tall trees.

ILLUMINATIONS

During my first year teaching I worked in the north county of Sussex in New Jersey. Before that time I didn't realize that farms existed within a hundred miles of New York City.

In the fall of that year one of my students invited me up his father's silo. I am not sure how this came about. Perhaps I said something in class about my farming ignorance; one of my bright seniors invited me for a tour.

I still see Brian sitting at the top of the silo's edge, urging me to climb the metal rungs embedded in the side of the three-story concrete cylinder. "Come on, Mr. de Vinck. The view's great."

The view was indeed great once I reached the top: hills of

corn and hay; the village church brooding like a white hen; a single road wiggling north toward the mountains.

"I like to come up here. My father wants me to be a farmer. This place, and the cows. You can hear the bells around their necks." Brian wore blue jeans, a plaid shirt, and cowboy boots. He was seventeen, in his last year of high school.

As I looked over the edge into the silo, I asked, "What would *you* like to do someday?"

"Well, I thought about college, a business degree."

"What's that smell?" I asked.

"What smell?"

"Something rotting."

"Fodder," the boy answered.

"What?"

"Fodder," he repeated.

My hands began to ache as I held on to the rough concrete rim.

"That's what we keep in here. It's a coarse composition: corn and other rough grains and bits of dried hay. The cows love it. Some of it begins to ferment when it's all pressed together in there. I don't even notice the smell. I've been around it for so long."

Rotting corn.

"Have you told your father about your college plans?" I asked.

"Well, my girl friend thinks I'm crazy giving up the land. That's what she called it. I've never been to New York, though they say the glow in the southern sky at night is the city lights. I've seen the aurora borealis, though."

"The what?"

"Don't you know, Mr. de Vinck? The aurora borealis? Each year my father and I drive up to Canada. It's always been 'our' trip. Once we saw these lights like metal waves shining against the night sky. My father said it's the sunlight from the other side of the world reflecting off the ice at the North Pole and bouncing into the darkness. I love my father."

"You'll find your own way, Brian," I said. "Most people usually do, those who ask the right questions."

"Questions?"

"Well, I suppose if you ask yourself questions that your inside voice answers, you'll know what to do." I attempted to adjust the discomfort in my body, trying to swing my right leg over to the other side of the wall to join my left leg.

"Don't do that, Mr. de Vinck. You've got to straddle the edge. You'll tip over one way or the other. I don't know how I'd get you out of the silo if you fell in, and it wouldn't matter if you fell the other way."

As I shook my leg, which felt numb, I asked, "How long have you lived here, Brian?"

"All my life. My grandfather started the farm. I've thought

about staying, or going to the community college and majoring in agriculture. My father points out the window and laughs whenever I attach a college degree to farming."

"I think between you and your father there's an answer. Let's go."

"After you. Watch out for the first step."

Brian and I climbed down the side of the silo. As we stepped upon the ground, I thanked him for the adventure. We shook hands.

Seeking out the lights of the city or the lights of the aurora borealis will lead to different illuminations.

THE REUNION

I was sitting on the living-room couch last night. Michael was sitting to my left; Karen was sitting to my right; David was doing his math homework at the kitchen table.

I was reading aloud Mother Goose: "Georgie Porgie, pudding and pie, / Kissed the girls and made them cry." It was nearly time for the children to go to bed.

"Simple Simon met a pieman / Going to the fair; / Says Simple Simon to the pieman, / Let me taste your ware."

The phone rang. "Humpty Dumpty sat on a wall, / Humpty Dumpty had a great fall."

"Chris," Roe called from the kitchen. "It's for you. Why don't you take it in your office? I'll finish reading to the children and put them to bed."

"Hey diddle, diddle, / The cat and the fiddle. Daddy has to answer the phone." The children laughed. "I'll be up to give you kisses."

Roe sat down with the children and continued to read. "Little Jack Horner / Sat in the corner, / Eating his Christmas pie."

I picked up the telephone receiver. "Hello?"

"Chris, this is Jim, Jim Dolen. Do you remember me?"

"Yes. Hello, of course I do." Jim had been the first person in our high school to wear bell-bottoms. He had been the best gymnast in the school's history. A star soccer player. I hadn't seen him in twenty years.

"I was speaking with a few classmates recently and we thought we ought to have a class reunion. We've never had one. Are you interested?"

"Mary, Mary, quite contrary, / How does your garden grow?" I could hear Roe reading in the background.

Twenty years. The high-school class of 1969: Jason's laugh, Cindy's kiss, Harry's Dodge Dart. Proms. *The Grapes of Wrath*. Jean Shepherd. Football games. Teachers.

"We thought," Jim continued, "that we would have a formal dinner. Should I put you down for a no, a maybe, or a yes?"

I loved my high-school years. It was there that I learned the power of telling stories in my English class. It was there that I laughed in my chemistry class as I sat next to Barbara Glynn. I knew the teacher liked me. I hoped Barbara did.

"Peter, Peter, pumpkin eater."

After our graduation ceremony in 1969, I remember driving alone in the car. I pulled out of the school driveway, turned left, drove down Hillside Avenue, and cried.

At first I promised everyone that I would stay in touch, but I didn't. I was deeply sad that those safe years fell apart. Some people run away from hurt. I have been running away from those innocent high-school memories for twenty years; the greater the distance, the sweeter the memories. And, besides, it has taken so much to become what I am today: husband, writer, teacher . . . father. . . . "Baa, baa, black sheep, have you any wool?"

I fear stepping back in time. Will Roe and the children disappear? Will I have to rediscover Walt Whitman and Emily Dickinson? Endure loneliness from the very beginning?

The ghost of Christmas past said to Scrooge, "These are but shadows of the things that have been. They have no consciousness of us."

To walk among my high-school friends, to dance with shadows of fading youth is to fall backward into a raging sea of disorder.

My wife and I have exchanged bits of ourselves: bone of my bone, flesh of my flesh. From the waters divided between us, our children were born.

It has taken me twenty years to arrange my life into patterns that seem to make sense. The poet Archibald MacLeish wrote that "the labor of order has no rest." I cannot stop now. I have a wife to embrace, students to teach, essays and poems to write.

The beautiful line of Robert Frost haunts me: "I have . . . miles to go before I sleep, / And miles to go before I sleep." I cannot return to my beginning. That is lost.

"Jim, put me down for a no. A class reunion would be too difficult for me to attend."

We spoke on the phone for a few more moments and then said good-bye. I placed the telephone receiver back in its carriage.

"Chris," Roe called from upstairs. "The children would like you to kiss them good night."

And the dish ran away with the spoon.

·3·

MARRIAGE

One man loved

the pilgrim soul in you.

— WILLIAM BUTLER YEATS

FIRST LOVE

Many years ago, when I was a junior in college, I was sitting in the first weekly seminar of the year. There were perhaps thirteen or fourteen students in class.

I remember looking around at all the new faces as we sat in a circle introducing ourselves. I didn't know at the time that a new and permanent element was to be added to my life.

There was this young woman. Her name was Jennifer. I liked her smile. She wore a light-colored blouse, blue jeans, hiking boots, a silver ring on her finger.

At the end of the class I drove home.

The following week I was sitting on one of the lounge chairs in the hallway waiting for the seminar to reconvene. Jennifer also arrived early.

I do not remember the first words we spoke together, but I do remember that we agreed to take a walk down the hall, down a flight of stairs to the candy machine.

At the top of the stairwell, there was a large picture window overlooking the campus, and Jennifer suddenly said, "I love windows." I know for sure those were the first significant words this woman gave me in our two years together.

I remember asking her what her name was. "Jennifer, Jenny, Jen. People call me different things."

"What should I call you?"

"Whatever you like."

I liked "Jennifer." It was always one of my favorite names. But her parents called her Jenny, so Jenny is what I called her too.

A writer does, indeed, need to have a muse. We all do, really . . . something that is rooted in memory, in desire, and in loneliness.

During the early years of my writing, the well I dropped my bucket in for inspiration contained the fresh waters of Jenny; today the water is cooler and fresher: Roe, our three children, the poets I read, the sound of my students reading aloud in the classroom.

Jenny was a part of those early beginnings where a human being realizes the power of mystery, sexuality, possibilities.

She was the very first part of my life where I dove off the high cliff into the raging sea below.

Before I met this woman, I didn't know I had to jump. We believe when we are young and secure that we can stay in the homes of our mothers and fathers forever.

I visited my parents last week. As I drove out the driveway, I turned and looked to my left at the front lawn. I spent many, many summer evenings of my childhood with my brothers and sisters playing kickball. There still isn't any grass growing before the tree that was home plate. I sometimes think that all I want to do in my life is return to those kickball games and wait for the sound of my father's voice calling us in for the evening as the first bats tip their wings above us in the near darkness of mid-July.

During the two years we dated, Jenny and I just held hands and barely kissed. Now I realize she was not in love with me.

I loved Jenny. I still do, the same way I love the poetry of Anne Sexton and Mary Oliver and William Carlos Williams and Wendell Berry. I love Jenny the way I love my memories, the music of Aaron Copland, the novel *A Tree Grows in Brooklyn,* all those things that splash upon the intellect, that moisten the heart and allow me once again to write for the evening.

This muse is not the memory of a single young woman. Our spirit is a collection of holy and innocent bits of the universe.

Only when Roe and I married did I become free. Only in my marriage did I understand what love is. Only in the birth of our three children did I understand the sacrifice of self for the survival of the other.

Bach, music, poetry, Jenny do not carry with them any risks. They are there to sail upon, to bathe in, to lie beside as the tide swells along the shoreline.

My wife, my children, they are what I have risked my sacrifice and my love upon. I have few chances in my lifetime to dare to love, and dare to embrace what is true. My wife is truth. Art does not return your love.

I haven't seen Jenny in many years. The very last time I was with her was at her new home in Long Branch, New Jersey . . . along the shore, those crashing waves.

She moved. I lost contact with her. I would someday like to see her again, and tell her about my family, give her a copy of my books, poems, and essays; I'd like to let her know what she meant to me. Perhaps she wouldn't understand. Perhaps she never really existed at all. Perhaps the midsummer night's dream isn't really filled with Shakespeare's Pucks and Oberons, and the forest fairies are just a combination of light and mist.

At night I toss and turn in the summer heat and squeeze my cool pillow.

LADIES AND
GENTLEMEN

Twice a year Roe spends a weekend with her six college roommates. Husbands and children aren't invited.

After the first night of her most recent reunion, I showered, dressed, fed the children breakfast, and stepped into our room to straighten up.

As I pulled the comforter over the pillows, I noticed a lump at the end of the bed. At first I thought it was the sheet wrinkled in a wrong position. I reached under the covers, felt around, and pulled out two rolled white socks.

Each night Roe crawls into bed with her socks on, and each morning they are rolled and loose somewhere under the covers.

Sometimes when I make the bed and Roe is curling her

hair I pretend that I am performing a magic trick and produce "Out of nowhere, not rabbits but two—yes, ladies and gentlemen, two—white socks." Only a wife would laugh.

When I was a graduate student at Columbia University, I used to visit many parts of New York City on my own: the museums, the plays, the festivals and bookshops. The worst place to visit when you are young and lonely is the zoo. It is difficult to laugh aloud by yourself when the peacock spreads out its feathers before you. And you can't stand by yourself before a cage and imitate the monkeys.

Michael asked me, "Did Mommy sleep in her bed last night?"

"No, Michael. Remember, she is with her friends at that farm in New York?"

"Is she coming home again?"

Years and years before I met Roe, I began to write poetry, because there was an emptiness deep inside me. I didn't want to have affairs. I didn't want to drink. I just wanted to be loved and embraced. I wanted to love and to embrace. Poetry filled the emptiness which, with patience and hope, transformed itself into the goodness and loveliness that is my wife.

"Of course she's coming home, Michael. Tomorrow afternoon. Let's make her a smiling-face card."

"OK. I'll use green."

When I found those white socks at the end of the bed, I began to sing aloud in the empty room, "Ladies and gentlemen! Out of nowhere, not rabbits . . ." And I stopped and remembered all the years before I met Roe and how lonely I was; I thought about the extra ten dollars she places in my wallet each week as a gift; I thought about how much I really like her voice on the telephone; I thought about how she reached for our first son after the moment he was born; I thought about all the meals she has prepared, all the laundry she has washed, all the students she has taught. I thought about the evening I asked her to marry me.

After she said yes, we stepped out into the college neighborhood and took a walk. We came upon an elementary-school playground. It was dark. We jumped over the fence, and we each took a seat on a swing. We began to rock back and forth, pushing ourselves higher and higher on the swings, and then we began to chant like children, "We're getting married! We're getting married!"

Today I stand before the peacock with my three children and with Roe and we laugh and laugh. And you should see how we act before a cage full of monkeys, my wife, my children, and I.

The children are asleep. Roe is home, ladies and gentlemen.

A green smile-face card is on the refrigerator.

ANNIVERSARY

On June 25 Roe and I will celebrate our wedding anniversary. She is sleeping as I write this evening. The children are sleeping. When a young man and woman take vows of marriage, they cannot see the patterns that are quickly placed before them: commitment, struggle, bills, children, goldfish, swing sets.

What is real to a newlywed couple is the wedding, the new place to live, the excitement of holy sexuality; but in the early days of a marriage there are also unnoticed hints of what is to come.

Roe and I flew to Paris for our honeymoon. As we were walking along a wide street, we saw a crowd in the distance gathering around some event.

The event was a street peddler selling plastic birds with cellophane wings. This yellow-and-red plastic bird flew around and around above our heads. To me it was like looking at the magic nightingale of all the fairy tales I had read. I thought it was wonderful. Roe was amused by my reaction to this toy. I called out that I would like to buy one, which the peddler was happy to sell.

My prize came in a long, triangle-shaped box with an illustration of the bird on the side panels. It acquired its power from a twisted rubber band which was connected to the wings from the inside to a small crank behind the tail.

After fifty or so turns of the rubber band, the bird was ready to be launched. Roe and I were too busy sightseeing during the day to try out my new purchase. That night, in the hotel room, I pulled the toy from its box, assembled its wings, attached the rubber band, and cranked and cranked.

Of course there wasn't any space to fly the bird in the room, so I just held it as the wings flapped up and down and up and down with great speed and power.

We spent the next five days walking through museums, up the Eiffel Tower, through the aisles of Notre Dame Cathedral. We circled the city in a boat.

One afternoon we were so hungry that we bought a loaf of

the real French bread. "Let's buy some cheese too," Roe suggested.

Our French was OK, but we weren't sure about weights and measures. Instead of buying a normal piece of cheese that would satisfy two people, we bought what turned out to be a mountain of cheese, nearly too heavy to carry, enough to feed all of Napoleon's army. We laughed as Roe placed our innocent purchase in her wide, deep handbag.

Afterwards Roe and I walked down into the subway. We sat on an empty bench waiting for the next train. We were nearly the only ones in the station. Suddenly a French policeman turned the corner, then another, then three more, then ten more. A pack of policemen were slowly walking in our direction. Their shoes were heavy against the concrete.

As we were looking at this advancing parade, Roe turned to me and whispered, "Do you think they're checking for cheese?"

We laughed and laughed, but very quickly sat in silence as the men in blue walked stiffly by.

A marriage is built upon love, yes . . . and commitment, yes . . . and sex and bills and children and goldfish, but it is also built upon seemingly insignificant moments that are shared between a husband and wife.

On June 25 I am going to bring home some terrific cheese for the children and I'm going to reach up into the bedroom closet, pull out a plastic yellow-and-red bird, bring the children to the back yard, and say, "Just wait until you guys see what this thing can do."

Roe will sit on the back stoop and shake her head.

"Do you think they're checking for cheese?" I'll call to her across the lawn as the children run after one of the greatest flying machines ever created, and Roe will laugh and laugh.

VOWS

My mother has two wedding bands on her finger: hers and her mother's. I like that, a link somewhere, gold touching gold. Although my grandmother died many years ago, her memory is still warm against the skin of my mother. From life to life.

Following our summer wedding, Roe and I moved into our two-bedroom home in the late fall of 1977. I remember standing on the front lawn and looking up at the small house. I thought to myself, Wonderful things will happen here in the years to come. I didn't know what things, but I knew they would be wonderful.

Something I also thought about quickly was the oak trees.

. . . Seventeen oak trees taller than the house covered the yard. Our street is called Woodland Court.

The township provides a leaf-collecting service. If we rake our leaves to the side of the road, they will come around with a vacuum-powered contraption attached to the rear of a truck and suck up the leaves. Roe and I missed the collection process that first year, so we had to rake the leaves, stuff them into plastic garbage bags, and carry the bags to the town dump.

I remember the leaves were wet and covered with ice by the time we had a chance to rake them. Roe held the bags open; I scooped up the leaves and dropped them into the bags. I didn't have gloves. We raked and raked. I scooped the leaves, dropped them into the bags, and blew into my cold hands; then we quickly returned to the raking.

One bag. Five bags. Fifteen bags. By the end of the afternoon we had forty large plastic bags filled with leaves leaning against the garage. A victory.

As we entered the house, Roe and I laughed, talked about supper, walked over to the kitchen sink, and began to wash our hands together. That is when I noticed my wedding ring was gone.

"When was the last time you remember having it on?" Roe asked.

"When we were raking the leaves."

The leaves. My wet, cold hands. The *forty* garbage bags.

"It must have slipped off while I was raking, or scooping up the leaves."

Roe and I spent over an hour walking back and forth across the lawn, bending down like chickens looking for bits of corn.

Then we both looked across the lawn at the forty bags, which seemed more and more like huge elephants that had just had a feast on wedding rings.

"We'll have to look through the bags," Roe announced. "We can't take them to the dump now."

"Let's have supper and worry about it tomorrow."

Well, tomorrow spilled into the next week, into the next month. Roe was teaching at the time. I was teaching at the time. We kept saying, "Tomorrow we'll go through the bags."

After four months the bags were under a foot of snow. One afternoon, when I was still in school, Roe decided to look through the bags in search of the ring. She was clever, thinking that I probably lost the ring early on in our raking, so she took the bag at the front of the line, dragged it across the snow and into the small side porch of the house.

Do you know what happens to leaves that are stuffed inside a plastic garbage bag for four months? They rot. They smell. They turn into a wad of ooze. Roe picked up a clump of fermenting leaves and sprinkled the remains before her as she sifted through the mess. Bits of stone, acorns, and sticks bounced against the wood floor. Each time something fell from her hands, she thought, Perhaps the ring. No ring.

Roe continued her search. Bag number two. No luck. Bag number three. No luck. Finally Roe gave up her system and just grabbed any bag from the patiently waiting line of bloated garbage bags, and, after she had jiggled the old leaves again and again, my wedding ring popped out onto the floor before Roe's startled gaze. She found the ring in the fourth bag.

When I came home from work that early evening Roe asked me how my day had gone. I asked her. We spoke. We laughed. We were preparing dinner together when I finally noticed Roe was wearing an extra ring on her finger.

"I found it," she said as she raised her shoulders a bit and smiled.

"You found it! I can't believe it! I thought it was lost for good!"

Roe took my hand in hers and whispered, "With this ring I thee wed," and then she once again slipped it onto my finger.

Gold touching gold.

·4·

FAMILY

Eden is that

old-fashioned House

We dwell in every day. . . .

— EMILY DICKINSON

BURIED
TREASURE

I just finished reading aloud *Treasure Island* to David. We began about two months ago. When his younger brother and sister were asleep, after they had had their turn listening to one of their books being read aloud, David and I sat on the couch. I would growl a good pirate growl, turn to the next chapter, and begin to read.

"Is John Silver good or bad?" David asked a number of times throughout the novel, for, of course, Silver was never the same person for more than a few days. Sometimes he was a scoundrel and other times he was, well, a little less of a scoundrel.

David and I traveled together through the streets of British towns, across the ocean in a fancy ship with huge sails. We saw the Union Jack raised and lowered, replaced by the Jolly Roger, upon that ship. We fought pirates together, David and I. We jumped when Billy Bones appeared. We felt a little sorry for the pirates as they discovered that the treasure was gone. We could nearly feel the weight of the gold Billy Bones hid in his cave as Jim Hawkins and his friends carried the loot onto the ship, which, finally, flew the British flag once again.

After we read the last page of the novel, I kissed David good night, and brought him up to his room. We said prayers. I adjusted his bedcovers; then I walked down into the basement and looked for a small wooden pirate chest I had when I was a child. It was about the size of a recipe box with a skull and crossbones painted on its top, a small lock, and a key on a string.

I found the chest. Then I reached deep inside my desk drawer for the gold coin, a Belgian gold coin, my grandmother gave me many, many years ago. I placed this coin in a small felt bag with a drawstring, walked upstairs into the kitchen and found in the cupboard a few pieces of butterscotch. The coin in the bag, the butterscotch—these were the treasures I placed in the small pirate's chest. Then I stepped outside in the darkness and buried the box in the garden under the mock-orange bush.

Can you imagine what it must have been like for a ten-year-old boy to discover a treasure map in his lunch bag, drawn by his father the night before? Can you imagine what it was like for this little boy as he followed the instructions on the map in his back yard—past the sandbox, past the swings, turn left five feet, and dig where you see an X? Can you imagine what it was like for David to find a real gold coin and three pieces of butterscotch hidden inside a brown treasure chest?

I hope that many years from now David will realize that the true gold is not in the treasure chest, but in the growl of his pirate/father, in the closeness of a small boy following along with the words in a book.

In the next few days perhaps you could buy a child a book and begin reading aloud and, if you come across Long John Silver, tell him David and I are waiting for him.

A DAUGHTER'S
QUESTION

I like to think about creation. I especially like to think about
those things which are created from an unlikely source. For
instance, icicles. Snow doesn't seem to have the capability
of transforming itself into clear, hard ice stems hanging like
fangs from the lip of a roof.

I like to place a diamond needle upon the grooved surface
of a round piece of plastic and hear, suddenly, Aaron
Copland's *Appalachian Spring*, or Bach's *Brandenburg*
Concerto.

I like to see the steam and mist rise from the sink and
collect upon the kitchen window on a cold winter evening as
my wife and I wash, rinse, and dry the hot dishes.

Who can really explain why things are created from a

mixture of heat and cold, or from one thing pressing against another?

I remember the Japanese flower shells. When I was a child I received twenty-five cents allowance each week. Often I spent it on two small shells which were closed together like a clam's. They were wrapped in a clear, stiff plastic. I haven't seen this type of shell in years.

The point was to break open the plastic bag, pick out the closed shells, and break the small seal which held the two shells together. Then the magic began. According to the instructions, I dropped the shells into a clear glass of water and waited. Slowly the two shells opened like two hands. From within, a small object began to float to the surface of the glass. As the water penetrated the small object, it slowly turned into a flower, a red-and-yellow flower.

What sense does that make? Stuffing empty shells with little paper flowers and selling them to children? Icicles do not make much sense. The creation of music from air being blown into empty chambers of brass and reproduced on a record all seems lunatic, but there is creation.

When each of my children was born, I had the same feeling . . . something lunatic, impossible, clear, diamonds, heat, shells, things rising to the surface. After all these years I still thank my wife for the children, still ask, "Where did they come from? How is it really possible?"

I remember an evening a few years ago when Karen was

five years old. She was draped upon my chest and shoulders as I carried her from the car and into the house. We had just returned from a visit to her grandmother's house. As I walked up the small front lawn through the darkness, Karen lifted her head, looked up at the full moon, and said, "Look. God put the moon back together again."

The next night, just before I kissed her good night, she asked, "Is there hay in heaven?"

"Well, of course there's hay in heaven, Karen."

"Are there donkeys too?"

"Yes, donkeys too."

"OK. Good night."

A little girl in the Northeastern section of the United States can inhale air with her lungs, exhale, speak about God, embrace her doll, kiss her father good night, and sleep. Isn't that lunatic, shells, ice, heat, mystery, mist?

KISSING THE
TOASTER

Before we can love someone, we must learn to love ourselves. Walt Whitman did not have any problem with that idea in his famous poem "Song of Myself":

> I celebrate myself, and sing myself,
> And what I assume you shall assume,
> For every atom belonging to me as good belongs to you.

The Greeks tell the story about the young Narcissus, who rejected the love of Echo the wood nymph. Of course Narcissus fell in love with his own reflection in a pool of water, leaned over to embrace what he saw, and drowned. Too much self-love is a dangerous thing.

One afternoon I was in the kitchen. Roe was visiting friends. The children were outside, hooting and laughing, whirling around the streets upon their bicycles as if they were circus clowns. As I looked out one window, I could see David lifting his feet up on his handlebars and coasting into the neighbor's driveway. Karen called out, "Look at this, you guys," as she quickly released her hands from her bicycle. "No hands! No hands! Bet you can't do that!"

Michael called out "Oh yeah?" as he flung his arms out and clapped his hands above his head. An impressive acrobatic feat if it were not for the training wheels attached to the rear spokes.

"Hey, that's not fair," I heard Karen singing in the fading distance.

I was alone in the house, so I thought it would be a good time to have an English muffin. I walked to the freezer, pulled out the frozen bread, and pried the two pieces apart with a butter knife.

The toaster was pressed back against the wall under the cabinet, so I slid it to the very edge of the counter, placed the two halves of the muffin in each slot, pressed down against the black knob, and waited.

I like to watch the inner coils of the toaster slowly turn from dark brown to that red glow.

After a few moments the muffins popped up and were ready

for butter. I also like the first taste of a muffin, especially when it is cooked to that light-brown, crisp stage.

The back door crashed open. "Mmmmmm! Muffins!" Karen called out. "Can I have one?"

I was caught in my solitude.

"Sure. I have to get one out of the freezer."

As I pulled the chrome handle of the refrigerator, Karen skipped past me. The coolness circled my hand with that familiar mist; I reached into the freezer. I was trying to pull a muffin out of the bag when I heard a loud scream. I turned to see Karen curled up on the kitchen floor sobbing.

"Ow! Ow! It hurts. Daddy, it hurts so much."

I quickly knelt on the floor and embraced Karen.

"Karen, what happened?" I asked between her weeping. All she managed to do was hold her mouth and weep.

Just above my head I saw the toaster on the counter's edge, and I saw two distinct lip prints. Karen had kissed the toaster, the still-burning toaster. As she came bouncing into the kitchen after her performance on her bicycle, she saw her reflection in the toaster and kissed her own image. I have seen her do this often while dancing before her bedroom mirror.

How would you explain to the doctor's nurse over the phone that your daughter has kissed a toaster? It does not give you much credibility as a competent father. Fortunately the nurse was not impressed. "I've heard it all," she laughed over the phone as we arranged for a checkup.

Karen sustained second-degree burns upon her lips, but they healed quickly.

Let us take delight in who we are. I applaud the scientific discovery that we all have unique fingerprints. I wonder if the same is true with lip prints.

I look forward to my little girl's wedding day, when she can confidently and publicly display her own beauty as a bride, and where she can announce her love for her husband with a ring, vows, and a kiss. At that moment I will remember holding her long ago in my arms, rocking her back and forth, as the two of us sat on the cool kitchen floor one afternoon.

There is a balance between self-love that is indeed a celebration and self-love that is tragic.

IN THE EYE OF
THE STORM

The children were nearly asleep when the wind began to brush against the top of the oak trees. There was distant lightning, and the sudden cool breeze at the windows. Roe sat on the living-room couch reading a novel; I tried to decide if I should read, write, or put the garbage out.

Then the thunder. The first summer storm and the children roared out at the same time. I walked up the dark stairwell as the quick blue flash danced around me.

"I'll tend to the children this time, Roe."

"Thanks, Chris."

I stepped into Karen's room first. She was crying.

"Daddy, I'm scared," she wept as she held her knitted doll made in Peru.

"That's OK, Karen. You can be afraid. Let's sit together and listen."

There were more bursts of light and the formal, aggressive thunderclaps which rattled the windowpanes. That is when Michael dove into my lap from his bedroom, carrying his blanket. "That was a loud one," he said judiciously.

"Yes, Michael. That was a loud one."

David stepped into Karen's room with an open book in his hands.

"Here, Dad, this will explain to Karen and Mikey all about thunder and lightning." David is always able to find helpful information in his bookshelf.

I took the *Golden Book of Weather* from David, and began reading aloud.

After I read, the three children and I looked at the illustrations on the pages; the storm outside our window flashed and roared.

Michael stepped up to the window and said, "Hey! Look what I found!"

What he had found was the flooded street. During every major rainstorm we have in our neighborhood, the street before our house floods, not enough to seep into the basement, but just enough to impress a little boy.

We all ran to the window, knelt down, and looked outside as the sky lit up again and again.

When we turned toward the room, I was convinced that the storm was nearly over.

"OK, everybody. Back to bed." Then *boom!* Even I jumped. "OK, everybody in Mommy and Daddy's room."

We all jumped on our queen-size bed. David stretched out to my right, Karen to my left, and Michael upon my stomach. As we lay there in the darkness, I thought about my grandmother and how much she had disliked the Fourth of July fireworks in America, and thunderstorms. She always said they both reminded her of what it was like in Belgium during World War II, when the night sky was illuminated with the flash of exploding bombs.

"Let's sing a song," Karen suggested.

"OK. I've got one I can teach you," I said.

"What do you get
When you gotta have somethin'
And it's gotta be a lot
And you gotta have it now?
What do you get?

Lick lack, snick snack,
Paddy wack, Cracker Jacks,
Ooooooo Cracker Jacks!

Candy-coated popcorn,
Peanuts and a prize,
That's what you get in
Cracker Jacks!'"

You would think that I was teaching the children the "Hallelujah" Chorus the way they took to the Cracker Jacks song. We sang it again and again between the exploding thunder and the lightning reflecting off their faces as we held each other in the darkness.

"Peanuts and a prize," they shouted.

Flash!

"That's what you get in Cracker Jacks!"

Boom!

The summers of my past had the same storms and the same rain and the same lightning. How could I possibly guess that the summers of my future would include two little boys and a little girl pressing their heads against my chest?

When the storm passed, just as suddenly as it began, I announced, "OK, everyone to bed."

"Thank you, Daddy," Karen whispered just before she kissed me good night.

"Thanks for bringing the book," I said to David as I folded his sheet under his mattress.

Michael fell asleep in my arms.

After I carried him to bed, I walked down the stairs. I could barely hear in the safe and holy distance a waning thunder. As I stepped into the living room, Roe looked up from her book and said, "That was quite a storm."

"It sure was," I answered. "It sure was."

FATHERHOOD

At midnight there was sudden and loud music blaring throughout our bedroom. Without asking any questions, I stepped out of bed, walked through the darkness, reached for the button on the clock radio on my dresser, and turned the music off. I slid back between the sheets and returned to my sleep beside Roe.

At two-fifteen Karen was staring at me eye to eye.

"The kitten is sleeping on my bed and I want to move my legs but I can't. The kitten is there."

Without asking any questions, I stepped out from under my covers, carried Karen to her room, and tucked her into bed. The kitten was gone.

After taking a drink of water from the bathroom faucet, I

returned to my room, slid between the sheets of the bed, and then slept.

At three-thirty Michael kicked me in the back and I woke. There he was, wrapped in his blanket, sleeping between Roe and me. Without asking . . . I lifted Michael and his blanket against my shoulder and carried him to his bed.

As I returned to my room, I jammed my right foot into the vacuum cleaner Roe had left beside the closet. I hobbled around in the darkness for a moment to work out the pain, limped back to bed, and then slept.

At five-fifteen I was awakened by the sound of a marble rolling back and forth in David's room. I passed the clock radio, made a wide step around the vacuum cleaner, and passed Karen's room; there, in the center of David's room, Mittens, our new kitten, sat and offered me a single meow.

Without asking any questions, I picked the kitten up, carried her to the kitchen, fed her, and pulled myself up the stairs and back into my bed. It was raining outside.

At six-twenty the alarm clock screamed.

Throughout the day at work I tried to figure out who had set the radio music alarm, why a little girl can't move her legs with a kitten on her blanket, how Michael had appeared in our bed, and why kittens have to eat.

We do not ask questions when our children (and cats) need us. We just do what we must. Questions come in the serious light of day, after the act of love. The answers are always vague, mysterious, and powerful: the warmth of a child against your chest in the middle of the night, a kick from a little boy under the covers, a single cat's-cry.

My right foot hurt all day, but I felt like dancing just the same.

A FATHER'S
ADVICE

Once I found a pink moth. Perhaps someone will tell me there is no such thing as a pink moth. There may be no such thing as a flying horse, or a gold calf, but I say once I found a pink moth.

The front door of the large three-story house where I grew up was protected on the outside by four panels of window-panes, nearly like a greenhouse. Before we entered the house, we had to turn into this small enclosure of glass, wipe our feet, turn the doorknob, and step into the front hallway.

I found my pink moth in this enclosure. It is here that birds often took a wrong turn and flapped their wings in a rush of feathers and noise against the glass, trying to break through the invisible barrier. It was here that spiderwebs collected, bees buzzed angrily against the glass as they too were caught in the trap.

One morning—perhaps I was eight, or ten—I stepped out through the front door. I noticed another moth was desperately trying to find its way out of the enclosure.

Each time I found a bee, a bird, or a moth trapped in the porch vestibule, I caught it and let it go. But I noticed this insect was a color I had never seen before on a moth: pink, completely pink. I caught the moth, held it in my cupped hands.

What does a boy do with a pink moth? I stepped back into the house, found a shoebox, filled it with grass and a soda cap of water, and placed my moth in the box.

It died, of course. Things cannot be held too long. They need to be set free. I threw the shoebox, the soda cap, the grass into the garbage can, and I buried the moth in the garden. I feel as though I am always being pulled between wanting to hold on to things and wanting to let them go.

I remember the afternoon Karen learned how to ride her bicycle alone for the first time. We began in the early fall, Karen and I. I took her training wheels off, but she insisted that I grasp the handlebar and the seat as we walked around the court.

"I'll just let go for a second, Karen."

"No!" she insisted.

Perhaps Karen will be a lawyer someday, or a singer.

Perhaps she will invent something, make a discovery, give birth to her own daughter. I thought about these things as we wiggled and rattled our way around the block. It didn't take her long to understand how to turn the pedals with her feet. As I held on to the bicycle, Karen's head and dark hair were just to the right of my cheek. She always looked down toward the front of the bicycle, calling out suggestions or laughing a bit.

After a few weeks Karen was comfortable enough with my letting the handlebar go, but I still had to clasp the rear of the seat.

"Don't let go, Daddy."

Halloween. Thanksgiving. The leaves disappeared. We spent less and less time practicing. Wind. Cold. Winter. I hung Karen's bicycle on a nail in the rear of the garage.

Christmas. One of Karen's favorite gifts that year was five pieces of soap in the shape of little shells which her mother had bought.

New Year's Eve. Snow. High fuel bills. And then a sudden warm spell.

"Roe?" I said as we woke up. "Do you hear that bird? It's a cardinal. It's been singing for the past ten minutes. Listen." Roe listened. I listened. The children were downstairs watching television.

After I showered, dressed, and ate breakfast, I found Karen in the garage trying to unhook her bicycle. In this last week of January, when it is usually too cold for the children to be outside on their bicycles, it was nearly sixty degrees. I walked into the garage and lifted the bicycle off the nail.

"I love my bicycle, Daddy."

She hopped on as I pushed her across the crushed stones of our driveway to the street. I gave her a slight shove. "Let go, Daddy!" And Karen simply wobbled, shook, laughed, and pedaled off as I stood alone watching her spin those wheels against the blacktop.

Einstein spoke about time, about the speed of light and objects moving beside one another. I wanted to run to Karen, hold the seat of her bicycle, hold on to her handlebars, have her dark hair brush against my cheeks. Instead I kept shouting, "Keep pedaling, Karen! Keep pedaling!" and then I applauded.

There is no use holding on to the pink moth and your daughter. They will do just fine on their own. Just set them free.

Keep pedaling, Karen. Keep pedaling.

·5·

CAREER

The labor of order

has no rest.

— ARCHIBALD MACLEISH

PIGEONHOLES

I have a theory about knowledge which has helped me explain the world and its people:

—There are people who think they know

—There are people who know that they know

—There are people who know that they don't know

—There are people who don't know

—There are people who don't know that they know

Which group of people do you belong to? Better yet, which group do you wish you were a part of?

I do not like being with people from the first group. They are arrogant and insecure. They must constantly impress us with their knowledge. They must always feel superior to everyone else. They never admit that they watch television or listen to anything other than classical music. They are snobs, status seekers, poor college teachers, lousy people to be stuck in an elevator with. And these people always look ugly no matter what size, color, or shape their eyes, nose, breasts, legs, lips, chin, waist, face, feet, hands are.

The people who know that they know are often people who don't need to broadcast their success. There is much conceit here too, but such pride is held as a secret to be worn as an invisible badge of self-congratulation. You won't find a poet in this bunch. A scientist perhaps, a lawyer here and there, a cook. Certainly generals and admirals are in this category. My cat also has a self-knowledge which gives her a certain poise as she licks her paws after a meal.

People who know that they don't know are perhaps most good college teachers, mothers, saints, devils, politicians (the honest ones), artists, and car salesmen.

Those people who don't know are most high-school and college graduates. They haven't had any sort of reading background or living background to know much of any use. These people are victims of commercials, political campaigns, and talk-show hosts.

The people I like the most are people who don't know that

they know. They are the ones who are humble. They work hard. They like the feel of sand against their bare feet. They arrive on time, laugh a lot. And these people always look beautiful no matter what size, color, or shape their eyes, nose, breasts, legs, lips, chin, waist, face, feet, hands are.

Of course, the trick is to define what it is that we know or don't know. That is the question, and, well, I simply don't know.

THE JUGGLER

I was sitting in my small office, a storage room really, where I am surrounded by old typewriters, stacks of soda cans, and old textbooks.

As an English Department chairman in a rural high school, I was assigned to this space, my work space. I call it my cave. There are no windows, but the custodians installed a silent ventilation fan in the upper left-hand portion of the ceiling.

During the times I am not teaching I am often sitting in my cave ordering books, adjusting the writing curriculum, filling out reports, preparing for class, or I am dreaming about becoming President of the United States, or perhaps Secretary of Education, or a juggler. They have an audience. They are in the news. Of course, I don't read much about jugglers, but they toss balls, or chairs, or flames into the air and people gasp. They are noticed.

When I was a freshman in high school, I admired a number of popular senior boys who walked through the halls before the first bell with their motorcycle helmets tucked under their arms. I liked the way they laughed together, these boys. I envied their confidence and the attention they enjoyed.

One afternoon during those years of adolescence, I walked home from school, ate a snack, and sat on the couch, where I found my brother's newest edition of *Popular Mechanics*. In the last section of the magazine, among the small advertisements for power tools and energy-saving devices, I saw an ad for the one-man Bensen Helicopter, which could be bought through the mail in kit form and assembled in your own garage in two weeks.

I built that helicopter in my mind again and again during my years as a high-school student, dreaming how I'd buy one of those motorcycle helmets, strap myself into the copter, hurl myself into the sky from the back yard. I'd fly over the school just as the buses were pulling up to the front doors. I dreamed about pulling the stick, balancing myself in the air above the trees, reducing power, waving to my friends, banking to the left, then to the right. I'd land on the football field, pop the strap from under my chin, tuck the helmet under my arm, and walk to my first-period class.

I became an English teacher. A department chairman. Honorable. Safe. Obscure.

For lunch today I brought a bagel and an apple from home. My tie matched my pants. I had to write a memo to my staff thanking them for their wise suggestions concerning the revised reading curriculum. I was grading a vocabulary quiz, just ready to bite into my apple, when there was a slight knock at my open door.

"Mr. de Vinck?"

"Yes? Who's there?"

I sit behind a filing cabinet which blocks people from seeing me as they enter. The room is so small that I must either leave the cabinet where it is or move out.

"Are you busy?"

I placed my apple upon the table.

"Kathy. No. Nice to see you. No, no. Come in." Kathy is in my second-period class. We had just finished reading Thomas Hardy's novel *Jude the Obscure* and begun a few days' review for the upcoming college SAT.

"I was outside with Eileen, and we found this leaf. She and I thought you'd like it."

An oak leaf: red, brown, hints of yellow, smooth and perfect as if it were cut for a jigsaw puzzle.

Kathy taped the leaf on the filing cabinet, said she liked Robert Frost, and then left.

To all young people I say, bring your teachers scarlet oak leaves and read Robert Frost.

Me? I'll continue to carry my books under my arms back and forth from my cave to the classroom. They are more comfortable to carry than helicopter helmets.

Perhaps I am a juggler, tossing novels and poems into the air. Kathy noticed. I'll be President some other year.

THE CHOICE

During my years as a high-school teacher I have often been asked to give home instruction to students who had broken legs, back problems, or any illness which prevented them from attending school for an extended period of time.

One morning a guidance counselor asked if I would be willing to accept another tutoring responsibility. "The boy's name is Roger. He has muscular dystrophy."

I took the assignment. That afternoon I drove to the house, which was surrounded by overgrown trees and shrubs to such an extent that it was difficult to find the front door. The gardens were filled with tall weeds and dried stalks.

Roger's mother greeted me at the door, welcomed me into the house, and introduced me to Roger. The boy was seventeen years old, shriveled, sunken in his wheelchair. His arms were as thin as his bones. He did not say hello. He did not smile. Roger had fallen into a severe depression. As I sat at his side and introduced myself, his brother, Doug, spun around the corner from the kitchen in *his* wheelchair, greeted me with a loud hello, and asked if I knew how to play chess. Doug, eighteen months younger than his brother, also had muscular dystrophy.

Although the two boys looked alike with their oxygen tubes attached to their noses, with their hands that looked like bird's feet, they were opposite in the way they looked at themselves and at the world.

Doug liked to build airplane models and talk on the telephone with his many friends. Roger watched television and spat. Doug always had a joke to tell as I entered the room for the day's lesson. Roger swore at me and asked that the shades be pulled down.

The more encouraged I was with Doug's gregarious ways, the more discouraged I was with Roger's pessimism and anger. Both boys had to be carried into their beds, drink their meals with a straw, have their heads pulled up. They both looked like insects: thin and brittle. Neither of them had the power to lift his arms. But Doug laughed and beat me at chess nearly each time we played. Roger told me often that people in his situation didn't usually live through their teenage years.

One afternoon I was alone with Roger. His brother had a

doctor's appointment. The lesson was progressing as usual. I read a story, then I asked Roger a few questions about the work. He refused to answer again. I reviewed a few new vocabulary words, but he sneered about the futility of learning anything in his condition. When I heard his mother's van pulling up the driveway, I knew it was nearly time for me to leave. Once again I tried to reach the boy.

"Roger, I have to go now. Do you hear the silence in this room?" I stood up, walked to the stereo, and turned the radio on to a selection of contemporary music.

"Now, before I leave I will have to pass the radio again. You can make a choice. Do you want me to leave the music on, or do you want me to turn it off? Like all the difficult things we must endure, we have a choice. Roger, there is a purpose for your wheelchair, a mystery." He did laugh here.

How do you teach wisdom and faith to a seventeen-year-old who is slowly dying before your eyes?

"It is something like music, Roger. Hear how it fills this room, gives everything about us a different meaning?" How could I teach this boy about poetry and courage?

"I have to go. Listen to the music. You have choices. Do you want me to leave the radio on, or should I turn it off?"

As I gathered my books and slowly stepped toward the front door, Roger turned his head and whispered, "Turn it off."

Harrison Salisbury wrote in his book *The 900 Days: The*

Siege of Leningrad about the grave hardships the people of that city had to endure during World War II as all supplies were cut off and nearly 1.5 million citizens were starved and frozen to death.

At one point during Mr. Salisbury's beautiful and painful account of the dying city, he explained how the electricity died and the radio station stopped its transmission. An old man walked to the station and implored: "Look here. If something is needed, if it is a matter of courage—fine. Or even if it is a matter of cutting the ration. That we can take. But let the radio speak. Without that, life is too terrible. Without that, it is like lying in the grave. Exactly like that."

During a particularly humiliating game of chess, humiliating on my part, Doug looked up and said, without provocation, "It's hard at night in bed when I'm against the wall." I didn't understand at first what he was saying. "I'm afraid of the darkness sometimes. It's too quiet. I call out for my mother."

Both boys are now dead. I spent two years with them every Monday and Wednesday afternoons with my collection of schoolbooks.

Did I fail them as a teacher, these boys, one who openly spat, and the other who called out for his mother in the middle of the night?

I wish Roger had asked for the music.

IGNORANCE

I was standing in my classroom one spring afternoon waiting for my next class to arrive. The air was warm. The windows were open. I stood in the sunlight and looked out beyond the fields.

Behind me I heard the desks being moved around, students entering the room, some calling out, "Hi, Mr. de Vinck," others laughing, some complaining about the quiz I had planned for the day.

My room was on the second floor, which overlooked the sidewalk leading to the outside student lounge. Students were walking below in a hurry, trying not to be late for their classes. That is when I noticed a boy who walked in an odd way, nearly bouncing on the balls of his feet. He was holding his books in an awkward manner, clutched against his chest as if someone were going to steal them. That is when I heard the low, steady chant: "You retard. You retard. You retard. You retard."

The first boy, a boy I recognized as one of the special-education students, was bouncing along the sidewalk. He was being followed by another boy, in a green shirt, who was calling out in a singsong mocking tone, "You sped! You sped! You sped!" Neither boy realized that I was watching all this from my open second-story window.

I *ran* out of my classroom. My students were startled. I *ran* down the stairs. My sports jacket flapped against my back as I slammed open the outside door.

The special boy turned and entered the building. The boy in the green shirt wandered off into the crowd of fifty or sixty students who were milling about the picnic tables before lunch.

Somewhere in the crowd. Perhaps to the left. Perhaps over here. Yes. There. The green shirt. I stepped up to the boy. I didn't know his name. All the air and anger that I could force out of my lungs I pushed out toward the boy, who at first turned and looked at me as if I were crazy. He jumped a bit too. I startled him.

"How dare you taunt that boy back there! How dare you call him such a name!"

"What are you talking about?" the boy smirked as he began to turn toward his friends.

My voice rose to a pitch I had never used in my life. "I was standing upstairs at my open window! I heard you! I saw the way you pressed your face directly behind that boy's head and laughed at him again and again, calling him a sped! *How dare you! Don't you know what you are doing?*"

All the students in the crowd suddenly stopped talking. I knew many of them. They had never heard me speak this way before. There was silence.

I looked at the boy. "My brother was retarded. He was blind and crippled. My brother was a 'sped' and I loved him," I nearly whispered. The boy in the green shirt looked at me, he looked at his friends, then he just walked away.

I turned to the students in the courtyard and quietly said, "His name was Oliver." Then I stepped back into the building and walked up the steps to my next-period class.

A MORNING'S
ATTITUDE

One morning, before I stepped into the building where I work, I heard in the distance the trumpets of Canada geese. The sounds were faint. I didn't know which way to turn. North? South? Against the rising sun?

East. They were flying toward me from the east.

I placed my briefcase to the right of the front door and stood on the sidewalk waiting.

The rural high school where I teach is surrounded by cornfields and smooth hills. There is a slow-moving rill along the side of the property down a small slope.

Because the sun was so bright, I picked up my right hand to shade my eyes. Against the new skyline I could just see a single dotted line in the distance. No, two lines. Perhaps three?

The trumpets gained in volume.

Stretched across the eastern sky was the longest, loudest chain of flying geese I had ever seen.

Do I dare become Icarus, and attach feathers to my arms with hot wax?

Only once did I dream that I could fly. I remember how the trees below me washed together into a soft green as I soared beyond my sleep.

I stood at the front door and waited for the geese to glide overhead. They looked as if they belonged in some prehistoric scene, in the virgin skies, perhaps on their maiden flight.

The sky belonged to the geese. Perhaps there were two, three hundred birds keeping up with each other, necks outstretched, wings beating—and the racket!

I pulled my head straight back. I could feel my hair against the collar of my coat. One of my colleagues walked past as I quietly said, "I've never seen so many at one time."

"Yeah, well, don't stand under them too long," he smirked as he stepped into the building.

I was sad to hear the joke. Did my colleague ever dream about flying? "But the geese," I felt like calling back, hoping he'd return and look up with me. "There are hundreds!" I wished I had said aloud.

I picked up my briefcase and gave a final glance at the distant birds fading beyond the fields and hills; then I too stepped into the building with my two heavy legs.

DREAMS OF A WEARY COMMUTER

There are certain times in our lives when we daydream about a different place, or a different afternoon, from the lives and afternoons we are at present living in.

When it is raining outside and the water rushes through the gutters, when I am driving home from work against the hard surface of the highway, when I have stayed up too late writing, I often think about the marsh of the Madawaska River in Ontario, Canada.

It is this river to which I have returned again and again as a child and now as an adult for my summer vacation; not just the river, but a very particular inlet. It is there I wade each year upstream from the cabin. It is no different from any other section of the shoreline, but this is the place I wish to return to when the common day rejects beauty and rest.

Each summer I pull the children along this side of the river. The rubber raft is their sea monster and I am their Poseidon, hauling them upon the clear surface of water as we laugh and laugh.

One late-August afternoon, as I stepped into the soft ooze and water, a blue heron leaped up before me like an exploding umbrella and disappeared beyond the trees.

I like to walk through the shallow river water and watch the minnows scatter in unison in quick, jerking motions. I like to bend over and look at my legs, which seem shorter in the magnification of the water. I like to sit on the moss that drapes the shoreline at the lip of the woods and feel the green texture against my hands.

Last year my son caught a bullfrog there. The year before that my daughter pulled a water lily out from the exact place where the bullfrog nearly escaped and pressed the flower in her hair, insisting, "Take a picture, Daddy!"

River clams, broken shells, smooth silt, and sand . . . trinkets the toll-booth collector would not accept as payment due on my long commute home each afternoon.

CHILDREN KNOW
BEST

If you wanted to know how I came to understand music, I would tell you about the morning I was driving to work and heard, for the first time, Aaron Copland's *Appalachian Spring*.

I define what I believe with examples from my life.

It is the same with my philosophy of education, which is based on those things that made a difference in my development as a person, teacher, and writer: children seek their own levels; children select what is of value to them; children learn from people they trust and love.

When I was in grammar school, I knew I did not measure up to many of the other children in the class. I remember Nina was a clever math student. Jerry was popular and quick and sure with a baseball. But I also knew I was brighter than Eric.

No one had to tell me I was poor at phonics and multiplication. Spelling was a mystery. And no one had to tell me that I liked to go into the woods with the neighborhood crowd and paint my face with mud and whoop and holler until dinner.

No one had to tell me I loved the sound of the geese or the sound of my mother singing "Silent Night" as she prepared dinner one evening. Children know what is around them. They know adults have power over them; they know cats have voices. Children also know, very early, that they will someday die.

When children feel the need to advance intellectually, they will just go ahead and make that step. I believe we give our schools too much credit for things that happen to children.

What schools do provide for children, however, is my favorite justification for what we call education: exposure.

Children sit in classrooms for thirteen years, and a whole troop of images, sounds, experiences marches before them. Books, teachers, songs all pass by on a conveyor, and children select what works for them.

If you placed in a line all the books I have read in all those years I've spent in schools, the line might stretch around my house. Many had no effect on me at all; some probably did things to me without my realizing what; but a good number changed my life: *Rascal; The Incredible Journey; The Scarlet Pimpernel; To Kill a Mockingbird; A Tale of Two Cities; The Grapes of Wrath*. The works of Loren Eiseley, Archibald MacLeish, Mary Oliver, Wendell Berry. I selected these books and authors along the way because they somehow matched what I am and what I hope to become. I was able to reflect upon my own experiences based on these books and draw conclusions about the world. That is learning. That is thinking.

My last assumption about education concerns children's abilities to learn from people they trust and love.

Children do what adults do. If parents smoke cigarettes, their children often wind up smoking. If parents are readers, there is a good chance that their children will read. Life imitates life. Our children look to us for any hints of themselves.

I had faith in my parents. I listened to Mr. Scaffuro as he told us second-graders all about Anthony the Ant, a wonderful, self-reliant insect who escaped danger with his wit and humor. I wanted to be Sydney Carton, the Scarlet Pimpernel, and Atticus. A teacher will be more effective if he or she is a person to admire, believe in, and love.

There are other things included in my philosophy of education. Somewhere there is a desire to teach children to distinguish between what is genuine and what is false. I know we are born with different abilities and limitations, but I believe we all have that unique something, a soul perhaps, that can be brought out by a teacher. We can teach children to have confidence in themselves. We can teach children to *see*.

·6·

LONELINESS

I am lonely, lonely.

I was born to be lonely,

I am best so!

— WILLIAM CARLOS WILLIAMS

ACCEPTANCE

Have you ever felt as if you were living with people who did not understand who you are? Do you ever ask yourself how it is that you see certain things while others around you do not see the same things?

I sometimes wonder if people see the same colors I do. Is a watermelon the same green and red in my eyes as it is in the eyes of others?

I know a woman who loves to paint. She also loves to sit on a certain rock that dips into the Atlantic Ocean. She acquires a sense of participation in the world of beauty when she buys a painting she admires and hangs it in her living room. She is married, has three children, weaves, sings to herself, and dreams about the possibilities beyond her world of the present. That world is a world dominated by a husband who doesn't understand art, doesn't care about rocks dipping into the Atlantic Ocean, and hangs mirrors and trophies on the walls.

When a woman looks in the yard and sees flowers, and when a man looks into the yard and sees the cost of fertilizer per square foot, when a woman enjoys a picnic, prepares a basket of ham sandwiches, wine, sweet cakes, and pickles and a man wants to make love in the grass every time, when a woman sees the world as a place that needs to be discussed, and shared, and a man sees the world as a place that needs to be accepted, and endured . . . when a man and a woman believe they have lost all that was possible between them, what can they do?

When a husband and wife find themselves in opposite worlds, there are a number of things they do: shout at each other until they die in their old age, or ignore each other. Many people do seek counseling; some talk to a close friend or neighbor about the impossible divisions that exist in their homes.

Perhaps the answer is in acceptance. We can fight and fight and fight about those things in our lives that don't seem to be exact, or free, or what we intended them to be, but there is a difference between fighting for those things that are truly important and those things that are truly selfish.

A man who does not have the ability to see the poetic force

the ocean tides have over a woman is a man who needs to be held even closer by his wife as she resists the wedge of perfectionism that constantly tries to slice between our imperfections.

From what I have seen in my life so far, there are many people who do not have the same ability to see beneath the surface of their own bodies and the bodies of their wives or husbands. There are many people who hide their true selves behind humor, talk about serious business or sports or the proper height a lawn-mower blade should be kept for best results.

Some people want to talk; others would rather read the newspapers. Some people want to hang colorful curtains on the windows; others would rather panel the basement walls. Some people want to be embraced; others want to build a deck off the kitchen.

A person who feels lonely after fifteen or twenty years of marriage, a person who feels lonely even though the house is full of children, a person who finds that the husband or wife will never learn about the beauty of a particular color in a particular painting is a person who discovers one of life's mysteries: we are all lonely, we all live with imperfection, broken lives, moments of great joy, and sadness. We all live through times when we question our relationships.

It is not the husband or wife who is at fault, it is not the jobs we are involved in, it is not the dreams or the money problems or the paintings or the ocean that lead many married couples to feel distant from each other at times. I believe it is the human condition to be part of a world of habit, structure, disorder, loneliness. But how we battle those forces, whether they manifest themselves in the people we love, in the art we admire, in the music we listen to, in the places we visit, determines not only the consequence of our being but also the triumph or defeat we, at the end of our lives, can present to our world as, perhaps, a piece of art, as perhaps a rock beside the ocean. We can become, each one of us, a single monument of endurance, love, compassion, in the acceptance of those things that cannot be changed.

THE SECRETS
WE KEEP

If you ask, I'll step down to my basement office and pull out my file marked "Poetry" and bring it to you. Better still, if you ask I'll bring it upstairs and read some of the poems aloud for you—not all of them, for there are more than eight hundred in my folder. I will read the poem about my father's barn and the one about the shooting stars. I'll read the poem I wrote about the boy who wandered around an abandoned house, or about the old woman in the nursing home who did not even remember the names of her children. There is a poem about an old woman who is speaking to her husband who has just died which I think you would like. I would like to read to you the poem about my neighbor's porch light.

Do you have something kept in a folder that you consider

to be a part of yourself as is your hair or voice? We think that we are known by the names we take, by the street addresses we have, by the places we work. But I believe there are things under our beds, in the closet, tucked deep inside a drawer or in the attic, that reveal more about who we are than all the rest.

Before my good friend John Moffitt, poetry editor for *America* magazine, died, my wife and I drove to Virginia for a visit. We did not know he was to be dead two months later.

John was one of the first editors to print my poetry. In the beginning of our many years of correspondence his letters were professional, to the point, making suggested revisions of my work or sending a brief note rejecting a poem.

But then something happened. His letters became more and more personal. He spoke about his niece, his childhood, his father. I began more and more to tell him about my struggles, my joys, my everyday living.

Friendship develops in a natural way, building upon what is familiar in each person, resulting in a new awareness that the person we embraced long ago could easily be a brother or a father.

"Roe, I'd like to visit John. Perhaps we could make a trip together? Leave the children with their grandparents? We could tour Washington, D.C., for a day, then drive out and spend the night with John?"

Roe thought that was a good idea. So did John.

He greeted us at the door of his little house. I was not expecting a white beard, a head of pure white hair. I was expecting a warm embrace, which is what Roe and I received.

John and I had been corresponding for four or five years without ever meeting. He played the piano for us: Beethoven. I read aloud some of my poems as I sat next to him on the crooked couch. He cooked us a dinner, showed us his irises in the garden.

Before we went to sleep for the night, John waved his hand toward my wife and me.

"Come here. Let me show you."

He led us to an ordinary pine cabinet with closed doors.

"Let me show you."

The cabinet was just our height. John reached over, pulled the handles of the cabinet, and opened the doors from the middle.

There before us were pink shells, yellow shells. Shells that looked like French pastry and horns. There were small scallops and a huge conch. All the shells were displayed upon a thick layer of cotton.

"I found many of them myself." He was laughing nearly like a child. Certainly the laughter was the sound of delight as he let us touch each shell.

"They are so smooth and beautiful, aren't they?"

When Roe and I left the next morning, John reached his right hand high about his head and waved good-bye as he stood before his house.

I never saw him again.

I think there are some irises still blooming each spring in Virginia. I wonder, sometimes, what became of John's seashells.

My poems still sit in my file cabinet. If you wish to see them, just ask. They are not pink or smooth, but I found most of them along the way.

Who we are is revealed in the secrets we keep.

SIMPLICITY,
SIMPLICITY,
SIMPLICITY

I knew that it was a mouse before I saw it run across the floor of the dark kitchen. I was reading F. Scott Fitzgerald's novel *The Great Gatsby*, in preparation for my high-school English class the next morning. It is a painfully beautiful book about a man who believed in a vision of beauty and hope which ultimately destroyed him.

Roe and the children were sleeping. The heat in the baseboard crept up from behind the couch. For the last three mornings we had been finding little bits of evidence that there was a mouse: chewed cookie bags, half-eaten crackers, small black droppings.

I was just reading the part of the novel where Jay Gatsby

announced with certitude that we can, indeed, repeat the past when I heard the crackle of stiff paper coming from the kitchen. Seconds later I saw a gray figure with a long tail run to the middle of the kitchen floor, stop, look in my direction, run back toward the cabinets, and disappear.

The world is so full of important concerns. Science tells us that, if we could catch up to the light that originated from the earth as it travels through space, and if we could capture that light, we could see images of the world's past: the launching of the first hot-air balloon at Versailles, Lincoln debating Douglas, the building of the Great Wall of China. The light from the kitchen couldn't project itself farther than the sandbox in the back yard. We have to determine for ourselves what is great and what is whimsy.

I was sure the mouse crawled into the bread-and-cookie drawer, which was partly opened. With the grace of a mime and the speed of a turtle I made my steps, then leaned forward and curled my fingers around the brass-and-ceramic handle.

One. Two. Three. I yanked open the drawer and there, in the right-hand corner, sat the mouse, all ears and eyes, gray fur, pink feet, and tail. For a moment it didn't move. It probably felt the way I felt as my wife caught me drinking milk directly out of the milk carton one evening when I was sure she was upstairs bathing the children.

Then my mouse leaped over the back side of the drawer and disappeared.

I quickly opened the bottom drawer, and there, under the plastic bowls and lids, I saw the tip of a tail. I yanked the entire drawer out of the cabinet and began carrying it to the back door.

Locked.

The mouse ran toward the cookie cutters and was prepared to leap again. I balanced the entire drawer on my left hand, twisted the lock in the door with my right, and, in a single motion, pulled the door open and nearly fell down the flight of stairs onto the grass.

The metal pots clanged. I laughed. It was nearly midnight and I was standing in my back yard holding the kitchen drawer in my hands. I hoped my neighbors were asleep.

At first I intended simply to dump the mouse onto the lawn, but I quickly understood that this creature could easily find its way back into the house, so I gently placed the drawer on the lawn and, one by one, lifted each item out until all that remained was the mouse.

I grabbed a plastic container and "Yah," I screamed. Bang. I slapped the bowl over the stunned mouse, slipped a lid under the upside-down bowl. Trapped. I was triumphant.

I carried my mouse to the car, placed him and the bowl next to me as I sat behind the steering wheel, backed out of the driveway, and then drove to the local church. I didn't think the pastor would mind if I released the mouse in the woods beyond the church.

The mouse scratched the bowl several times, ran around a bit. Stopped.

I pulled the car over to the side of the long driveway leading up to the church, stepped out with my mouse, and knelt upon the grass. A man and his mouse at midnight.

After I tipped the bowl forward, after I popped off the lid, the mouse gave a terrific jump, leaped before the headlight of my car, and bounced nearly like a kangaroo down the road, heading toward the rectory.

Often the smallest things can lead us to hidden adventures and simple delights.

ADRIFT IN A
MOONLIT
KAYAK

"Let's take the kayaks out on the river," my brother-in-law Peter suggested as my sister Maria, Roe, and I were peacefully sitting on the couch in the cabin while the three children slept.

Peter has acquired his helicopter license, surfs, scuba-dives, and flies kites, boomerangs, and model airplanes; he hikes, plays tennis and Ping-Pong, can build and repair anything, understands math and science better than most.

"Let's take the kayaks out," he repeated with less hope in his voice.

It was nine-thirty in the evening. I wanted to sit and eat potato chips and talk ourselves into sleep.

Peter sat beside us in silence.

My idea of a vacation is to sit and read or talk after a full day of picking berries with the children, and swimming, and swatting mosquitoes, and walking to town for ice cream. Perhaps Canada ought to pass a law: once the children are in bed, you are allowed to sit, read, and talk in peace.

I looked over at Peter as he gave me this grin which meant "kayak-river-fun."

"OK. Just for a while," I relented.

Peter dumped his chips back into the bowl, and headed for the door.

"Shouldn't you take a flashlight?" Maria suggested. "It's completely dark out there, especially on the river."

Peter waved his hand quickly, drawing me out of the house.

"If you guys don't bring a light, at least keep away from the middle of the river," Maria called out as Peter and I, like boys at camp, ran down the narrow path toward the beach.

"This is going to be great! I'll take the yellow one. It's a bit tricky to manage," Peter warned. I had never been in a kayak before.

After Peter pushed his vessel into the water, stepped in, balanced himself, and slid into the seat, I did the same thing.

"Let's go across the river," Peter suggested.

"What river?" I asked.

"It *is* pretty dark," Peter said with a slight chuckle.

We began to propel the small boats. It was effortless. All

we had to do, it seemed, was dip the paddle into the still water and the kayak slid forward.

As we worked our way through the darkness, Peter and I began talking. He told me about his father taking long kayak camping trips. I told him how my father built sailboats without any power tools.

When we reached the middle of the river, we both stopped. As we floated silently side by side like decoys, Peter noticed a glow just beyond a distant hill.

"The moon!"

As we continued our conversation, the coy moon stepped out from behind the curtain of darkness and danced upon the river.

"I hope to have a close relationship with my children when they are older," I said as I watched Peter's dark silhouette pass before the low moon. He looked like a model for any Eskimo folk art.

"Chris?"

"Yeah?"

"Do you hear that?"

"What?"

"Sounds like a motor," Peter said.

"Yeah, now I hear it."

It was, indeed, a motor approaching upriver.

"Any suggestions?" I asked.

"Yeah," Peter said with that same chuckle. "I think we should have brought a flashlight."

I thought about those movie scenes where the large black bow of a ship crashed over the small, helpless dinghy floating in the sea's darkness.

The motorboat was approaching. Closer. Closer.

"I think it's coming from the right," Peter whispered.

"Nah. I think it's heading straight for us."

Closer. Closer. Putt . . . putt . . . putt . . . A red light blinked on and off to the right and the motorboat slowly edged passed us.

"It was a lot closer than I thought," Peter laughed as the kayaks wobbled back and forth over the motorboat's wake. We both laughed.

"Look at the stars' reflection in the water!" I said.

Peter and I watched the stars' light wiggling against the dark water; then we pushed ourselves back to the shore.

As we walked back along the path toward the cabin, we could see Maria and Roe still sitting on the couch talking. I howled like a wolf.

I'm glad Peter invited me out in the darkness, where the moon and stars and grown men play. I'm glad Peter is my brother-in-law.

GIFTS

Each November for the past eight years, I knocked on the door of my neighbor's house and asked him if I could borrow his twenty-four-foot aluminum extension ladder so that I could clean out the autumn leaves from my gutters.

Each November, Barry would pull on his plaid coat and his work gloves, and escort me out back behind his house, where he kept the ladder under the crawl space.

The two of us would stoop down and make our way through old cobwebs, reshuffle a Big Wheel or two, drag a hose out of the way.

"Are you going to your folks' home for Thanksgiving this year?" I'd ask.

"Same as last year," he'd answer.

Barry would grab one end of the ladder and I'd grab the other end.

He and his wife, Patty, came to the baptisms of my children, and handed down pants, shirts, boots their children outgrew. Each Christmas, Patty sent over the best homemade gingerbread men I have ever eaten.

"Let me help you get this thing over," Barry would say as I'd jump over the thin wire fence which separated our yards. The ladder wasn't really heavy. We just enjoyed playing out our roles in the neighborhood.

"I really should buy one of these things."

"Why bother?" Barry would say. "You can use it anytime."

Barry and I met for lunch once at his company dining room, which overlooked Manhattan. His treat. My family and I sat in his house for five or six hours while the oil company came to repair our stalled furnace one February night.

"The pulley system sticks a bit. You might want to grab hold of the rung as you extend the ladder."

"I'll get it back in a few hours."

"No hurry. If I'm not home, just leave it on the other side of the fence," Barry would say with a quick wave as he'd return to his house.

Each November.

This past spring, when the "For Sale" sign appeared on Barry's front lawn, it was difficult for me to accept that his company really was leaving New York City for Dallas.

As people began to arrive with the realtors, even when the moving van stood before Barry's house, I still didn't react as I should have. When events play themselves out to an inevitable end, I tend to stand back and observe.

On the day he and his family left, I should have embraced Barry. I simply shook his hand and said goodbye. As he drove down the street, I should have waved and waved and waved, but I didn't.

In the early evening, as I was pulling my son's tricycle in for the day, I found, leaning against the side of my garage, the twenty-four-foot aluminum extension ladder.

A PERCH USED TO
VIEW THE
WORLD

From what place do you stand and look out upon the world? I remember a girl I was dating in college who led me to the top of the New Jersey Palisade Cliffs. She and I stood side by side as we watched the Hudson River below us carry a barge under the George Washington Bridge. We could almost stretch our hands out above all Manhattan at one time.

One afternoon during those college days I drove to Bear Mountain Park in Harriman, New York. I was alone, puzzled about this loneliness, unsettled about the future. I left the car in the parking lot and began to climb up to the peak of the mountain. As I was taking my final steps, I pushed a branch aside and discovered a man sitting by himself on a rock. He wore hiking shorts, hiking shoes, and a gray shirt.

At first we didn't say anything. I just stood a few feet

away from him. He must have been in his early sixties.

"If you look hard enough," he finally said, "you can see clear into Connecticut."

We were standing upon one of the highest peaks in the metropolitan area.

"Yes, it is very beautiful," I answered.

"I'm from the city, the Bronx," my new friend said to me. "I come here once, sometimes twice a month. You can walk all day here, like holding the whole planet in your hand." Before us we could see miles and miles of the Catskill Mountains like a bulging, smooth carpet.

"Look at that hawk spinning down there," I said.

The older I get, the more I see there are places we can return to where everything can be observed in a single glance.

I think often about my good friend the poet and novelist May Sarton. She writes on the third floor of her York, Maine, house in a room which overlooks the ocean. There is something wonderful about this vantage point, looking down at the shifting tides, looking in a southerly direction to all America below the state line. May just has to peer over her typewriter and all is there waiting for her: the cat in her garden, the snow, the ocean, the whole country in one single embrace.

One afternoon in 1964 my mother was taking a rest in her room. Somehow three or four of us children found our way onto her bed as she sat there propped up on her pillow. (So much for a mother's rest.)

The subject of the World's Fair came up. My mother sat there in her shawl and told us about the wonderful World's Fair she saw in Europe when she was a girl. She explained to us all about the flags, the foreign costumes, the exotic foods, the music. She laughed as she described the modern inventions, and the wonderful parades. Sitting on my mother's bed while listening to her describe the possible magic we were soon to see at the New York World's Fair was like sitting on a flying carpet and looking down upon all that was fanciful and mysterious and good and possible in the world.

It turns out that one of my most favorite events of the fair that year was the dance of the Belgian men in their tall feathered hats, in their embroidered costumes, as they twirled about the streets holding small lamplike baskets filled with oranges.

We do not have to place ourselves at the peak of a mountain to embrace the world. We are not Napoleons bent on conquering the universe. We are all, simply, poised upon our own unique platform: a room, a state park, a mother's bed. We all can observe what spins around us: barges, hawks, the ocean, men dressed in fancy suits swinging baskets of oranges at their sides.

I keep all that I have seen in my memory, which is, ultimately, the final perch to point down from and say at the end of my life either "yes" or "no."

I vote yes.

·7·

LOOKING BACK

. . . the past to the future—

which is of course the miracle—

which is the only argument there is

against the sea.

— MARY OLIVER

AN IMPULSE
IS GIVEN

No one really knows why the Stone Age people thousands and thousands of years ago crawled into deep caves and painted horses, deer, and large bulls upon the solid rock walls. Some anthropologists suggest it was a religious ritual, an explanation to the gods, retelling to them, in human terms, the boundaries we keep in order to continue living.

I have seen these paintings in the caves of southern France. Is it possible that a man crushed the roots of common plants and carried these dyes with him into the hollow earth? Is it possible that he held a flame before him? What did this man believe as he stood alone deep within the earth, which was cool and moist and silent? How did he decide where to begin?

Why draw a horse or a deer? Did he talk while dipping a stick or his finger into the colors and tracing the outline of a wild cow upon the wall? Did he sing? No one knows.

As I look around the room where I write, I see on the wall a reproduction of a Russian icon of Christ looking toward his right. Before me are three happy angels painted by an unknown German artist. I keep a framed five-inch portrait of Charles Dickens and a portrait of a woman by Leonardo da Vinci.

We like to adorn our walls with photographs, posters, memories, or visions of a finer place. I like the idea of placing a border around something beautiful, as if beauty can be caught.

When my brothers and sisters and I were children, my grandfather offered any one of us a dollar if we could catch the rabbit which appeared at the foot of the raspberry bushes each afternoon. The idea of sneaking up on a rabbit, trying to leap out and embrace the wild creature with my two arms, always appealed to me. Do the astronauts have this same feeling as they circle the earth around and around, as if they could lock their arms around the entire world and carry it off with them, to their grandfather's delight?

During the first three years of my marriage, my desk and books were arranged in the spare room in our two-bedroom house. When my first son was born, I began to clean out the basement. I swept the floor, moved old tools and pipes into the garage. I was going to finish the basement so I could have a new place to write.

A neighbor advised that before I framed out the studs I ought to paint a sealer upon the rough surface on the cinderblock walls to keep the moisture out. This is what I did.

The sealer was white. The walls were prepared. The studs were in place. I was about to lay the first piece of sheetrock in place when I felt like singing.

I took a Magic Marker from my toolbox, faced the south wall, and drew a bow and arrow, stick men running, a wild horse and a deer. Next I printed the poem I had finished writing the night before upon the white surface of my wall, and then I covered the entire wall with sheetrock.

No one knows there is anything behind the wall.

NASA left a plaque upon the surface of the moon. Before my grandfather died, he insisted that a rose trellis be constructed in the back yard. A man in the year 15,000 B.C. crawled upon his knees, carried a grease-burning lamp in one hand and a collection of paints in another as he worked his way toward a rite or an impulse given to us human beings alone among all creatures.

I think God is interested in how we respond to sadness and joy, to death and to life. That response is seen in our museums, in our photo albums, in the things we frame upon our walls. That response is painted in deep caves and drawn upon the cinderblocks of a house in the suburbs.

We alone among all creatures look around at our children, glance at the shadows, listen to the sounds of the neighborhood, and laugh, or sing, or weep.

SWIMMING WITH THE
SEA TURTLE

Lately I have been thinking about the sea turtle. As I restlessly lie in bed, as the distant streetlight gives the dark room a deep-blue shade, I think of the sea turtle I saw at the Baltimore Aquarium a few weeks ago.

Roe, the children, and I took an overnight trip to the aquarium. We laughed at the sea otters. We pressed our noses against the thick glass and watched the whales swim before us, gliding through the invisible water as if they were giant ghosts.

On the top floors of the aquarium, there was a tank of water that encircled an enormous room. The tank was perhaps two or three floors high. That is where I saw the sea turtle swimming around and around the room as if it were held to a kite string. It never lost its stride, giving the water regular heaves with its fins.

I walked alongside the turtle for a few minutes while the children ran to another exhibit. We two kept an even pace, the turtle and I.

My sister Anne taught me how to swim. "Just hold your nose and go under, Chrissy, like this," and Anne would leap from the wall of the township's summer pool and splash into the water and disappear into the white foam. Then I would see her swimming underwater like a frog, kicking her legs, extending her arms before her, and popping out several yards away. "Now you try it!"

Anne and I swam under each other's legs, raced back and forth between the raft and the blue wall, stood in line at the white ice-cream truck.

I had never walked alongside a sea turtle before. He was to my left. The aquarium was crowded, so I had to weave in and out between the people to keep up with the turtle. He just kept pressing the water with his fins, maintaining the same rhythm.

I sometimes feel like this turtle, trapped in a round existence, swimming in the day's routine, never losing a single beat of my arms. Each morning I wake up at six-fifteen. Each afternoon I have lunch at the same desk. The evening paper has the same ink, the same shape; after a while even the stories are the same.

Sometimes I would like to swim in the opposite direction. Sometimes I would rather not swim. Sometimes I would rather not be the turtle, but be the otter, rolling myself in sea kelp and laughing.

Around and around and around I go in my circle as my children watch me each day, as they walk beside me each day, as they watch how I swing my arms, twist my neck, turn, and look at them.

Sometimes I wish I could be thrown back into the sea and simply swim again with my sister Anne. Once we pretended we were pearl divers chasing after our ice-cream nickels, which we dropped to the bottom of the concrete pool.

When you are in bed at night and you are restless and cannot sleep, what do you think about? Lately I have been carrying a sea turtle upon my back to the Maryland shore, slipping into the water, extending my arms, and teaching the turtle how to swim in a straight line all over again: "Just hold your nose and go under like this," and I press the cool water with my bare arms and then I sleep.

THE DAY THE ELEPHANT TREE DIED

Something is always at the center of our lives. For me it is my wife, my children, and my writing. When I was a child, I didn't know the world revolved around my mother and father. They revolved around me with their arms, the voice of my mother telling me that it is good to be grateful, the presence of my father working day after day without a complaint.

It is an odd thing to look back to my childhood and see in the distant memories things that seem, today, not so important, but there once were against the silver banks of my youth rivers of liquid gold, that place where the birds did sing all afternoon.

In the middle of the yard there was an apple tree. It began at the base as a steady, thick trunk, but then it took off in three directions: a thick, long branch to the right, a thick, short branch to the left, and a few thin, full branches toward the sky.

Whoever climbed the tree when I was a child owned the tree for the moment. I remember when I was finally old enough to jump into the center V where the branches met, the wide V in the tree that was, for me, the wide saddle of a large gray elephant. I rode to Africa and back, or to Kansas, upon the hump of the elephant tree.

It took particular courage to step out upon the extended branch to the right and walk its entire length, as they do in the circus, high above the audience, without a net below . . . just my grandmother gathering the apples I'd shake to the ground. We had many jars of apple sauce in those autumn days thirty years ago.

One fall afternoon a cow escaped from the neighbor's pasture and was discovered eating apples at the base of the tree. I remember climbing up into my saddle and pretending that the cow was a mad bull, or Paul Bunyan's blue Babe come to visit, and I in my high command herded the grand creature back to his home.

I remember the wooden sword my father made for me, and how it fit into the loop of my belt and how I'd stand upon the top branch of the apple tree, wave my sword above my head around and around, and shout a victory whoop which I did not understand as my grandfather called across the yard, "Be careful, boy, up there."

One morning in July, when I was a teenager, my mother and father, my brothers and sisters pulled out of the driveway in the white Ford station wagon and headed north to our two-week Canadian vacation. It was my turn to stay home with my brother Oliver . . . blind, crippled, retarded Oliver.

It had rained and rained during the night. When I had waved good-bye to my family, I turned into the house. The air and ground were damp. There was still a thin mist in the distant woods.

As I entered the house, I heard a sudden, tremendous crack, a collapsing rush of sound.

I ran to Oliver's room. He was in his bed as usual, quiet and at peace. I looked out his window and there, beyond the mist, was the apple tree on its side in the yard like a beached whale or some green, deflating hot-air balloon. The weight of the years and the rain had pulled the tree to its side and to its death.

In the center of our lives we find our wives and husbands; we find our children, our parents, a particular day, letters, pictures, memories.

I have made my peace with the adult who I have become,

taken on the responsibilities of love and the labor of being a husband and a father. I accept my vocation as a writer, pray for strength each morning, and sometimes wish I could find that sword and climb upon my gray elephant and chant, once again, "Victory! Victory!," which I do, now, understand.

IN THE BEAUTY OF
OUR STILLNESS

I was browsing through the local library just for fun: maga-
zines, the newspapers, over to the book stacks. I sometimes
like to leaf through an atlas and measure the distance between
my house and Belgium, where my mother and father were
born.

On this particular afternoon I wandered toward the over-
sized books: large picture books, nature books, books on
posters and photographs. I picked up one book that seemed
as large as a tombstone.

I sat in a chair and began turning the pages: one page,
one page, one page. This book was a collection of photographs
taken in the 1920s: the cars, the buildings, people, children,
all held in their stillness in black and white.

But then there was a picture of a young woman. Her long hair was held up above her neck with a clip. She wore a long, pleated dress. She sat upon a rock overlooking the sea. I can still see this woman's face: a softness to her skin, features belonging to youth and poise and summer.

Like a fossil from my back yard, reminding me that the ocean once rolled over the very ground where I now write, the photograph of this young woman contained a universal form, like the universal form of the shell, whether that shell is discovered upon the beaches of Sandy Hook, New Jersey, or along the lips of the Mediterranean, or embedded in a cracked rock in my driveway.

I heard once about a people who were frightened of photography for they did not want their spirits held captive inside the box of the camera.

Stop the heart and the body dies in a particular moment in time, at a particular breath, in a particular motion.

Did you ever press the imprint of your hand in wet cement? Did you keep a particular hat or dress you loved once which reminds you of other times? Do you remember the shape of your first home?

The geometry of our lives can be calculated by different shapes that fit together and that do not fit any longer. The space we can no longer fill and the space we fill today determine where we are.

The person you were is not really the person you are today,

though there linger, still, shadows, hints, a slight tone of voice that does borrow from the past.

The woman in the library photograph is perhaps ninety years old today. Perhaps she died long ago. Who was she? Did she fall in love with the photographer? Did she swim that day? Did she ever marry? Write a book? Snap green beans? Did she like jonquils? She was a form of beauty. Her spirit was, indeed, stolen for a moment and held captive upon the photographic paper.

What image of yourself do you leave behind for your children and lover? What is the pose you hold in time for some stranger to look upon who wants to join you there on the rock beside the sea?

AUTUMN BOYS AND
ACORN PIPES

Deep in the center of the woods (all woods have a deep center)
there was a ring of gray stones, the campfire, which is what
my brothers and sisters and I called it.

To the left of the fire pit a tall tree, which shot up into a
V, leaned away from the clearing in the woods. To the right
there was a small crab-apple tree which was good for climbing. Surrounding the trees and the circle of stones were low
bushes of red berries which we picked in autumn and strung
together with sewing thread and wore around our necks.

It was always Bruno, my oldest brother, who had the idea:
Let's bake some apples in the woods. I was the first volunteer
to hunt for the aluminum foil, the butter, the brown sugar,
and the apples which were always in the white kitchen drawer

in October. It is in the act of creation that I find some of my greatest joy.

I liked to watch my brother lift the largest apple from the paper sack. I liked the feel of a stem between my fingers as I reached in and grabbed my selection. I liked to watch Bruno dig out the apple cores with a knife, pack the insides with butter and sugar, and wrap each in aluminum foil ready for the open fire.

The closest I ever came to actually flying under my own power was during those days when Bruno carried the apples down the lawn toward the woods. I ran out the back door, jumped down the green porch steps, ran against the back lawn, leaped over the wall into the garden of wilting marigolds, and joined Bruno just as he was about to step past the jewelweeds and disappear between the trees.

As we reached the camp, the house disappeared, the sky disappeared. Only my brother and I seemed to exist as we gathered dried sticks and oak leaves. Just before he lit the match, Bruno placed the two apples in the center of the stones, in the center of the firewood. Seconds later quick flames danced in a yellow wiggle from place to place, until the silver-cased apples were surrounded by heat and smoke.

"Let's make pipes," I suggested as we waited for our meal to cook.

Bruno and I stepped away from the fire and began searching the ground for the largest acorns we could find. After selecting two plump brown ones, we took out our five-and-dime pen knives, which were the size of our thumbs. I remember trying to pull out the small blade with my fingers until I leaned over, held the exposed side of the blade in my teeth, and pulled.

"You're going to cut yourself, you silly goat," my brother said.

After we popped the caps off the acorns, we dug out the insides with our knives, then pierced each acorn's belly and pressed a small, thin stick through the hole.

I remember how we leaned back upon a tree trunk with our new pipes in our mouths, as smoke rose from the fire and brown sugar hissed in the heat.

Outside, above the front door of the house where I now live, there is a carved shell. I do not know why it is there. Was it a whim of the carpenter during his lunch to carve a bit of wood he found beside his legs as he stretched out upon the earth which is now our front lawn?

I like the dot of the letter "i."

My daughter recently returned from school with a picture of her favorite food, a tomato, which she had drawn in the center of her rough, cream school paper.

I admire the hawk which can swirl around and around high above the earth at a great distance and spot a mouse or a rabbit running hundreds of feet below against the dried grass.

A poet's job is to take the large, universal things like the sun and sadness and bring them down to the ordinary world of a common existence. It is also the poet's job to take the very small things and extend them outward into greatness.

Hold the sun in your hands. Weep into the open palms of those you love.

Observe the letter "i" and the tomato upon my daughter's paper. Come to my home and see the wooden shell; admire the hawk's vision. Join me as we strain our eyes together and focus back over time, and part the top of the tall trees and peer down and see two autumn boys eating baked apples with melted sugar.

See how the smoke rises up from the center?

THE BEAR

Many years ago my father purchased some property in Ontario, Canada. Much of the land was cleared for farming, though we were not farmers. For years the open fields rested upon their backs, waiting for us to roam upon their bellies. Each summer vacation, for two weeks, you could hear us children laugh, or perhaps it was the earth that laughed.

I remember Bruno showing me the lichen growing in the grass. It was a clump of grayish-blue material like a sponge with little red caps at the tip of each column. We called them "wooden soldiers" and always gathered a handful for the windowsill back in the cabin.

I remember eating wild raspberries, which grew along the edge of the path. I liked to pluck the berries one at a time until my cupped hand was full, then press them all at once into my mouth. I also remember the taste of a small beetle I hadn't seen hidden beneath the pile of raspberries.

Sometimes my sisters and brothers and I would pick the black-eyed Susans and weave them into crowns, or we would hunt for quartz crystals and drop them into our pockets to be washed and admired later that evening.

And if the day called for an adventure, my father took us children through the open fields, up the hill, past the beaver pond, through the gate to the "secret place."

I do not know who discovered the secret place, nor do I know who gave it its name, but it is a place which remains in my memory, and it is still a secret, because no one knows about this except my parents, and my brothers and sisters.

North of the beaver pond, beyond the fence, to the right of the first field, there was a thick grove of pine trees. To the east, through the trees, the branches scratched our faces. The sunlight was cut off more and more the deeper we entered into the woods. But then, suddenly, we came to a light beyond the trees, a brightness that ought not be there.

In the center of the pine forest there was an open circular "room." The pine trees formed tall green walls which completely enclosed this room.

Many years later I came to understand that the room had a simple, natural explanation. A large, flat boulder was embedded just below the surface of the ground so the pine trees could not take root above the large rock, but there was enough soil for wild grass, which created a thick carpet for children to fall back upon and dream about Robin Hood and all the hidden places deep in Sherwood Forest.

One summer a local hunter told us that there was a bear who had taken residence somewhere on my father's property, and that was the summer the fields, the bushes, the secret place all closed their doors to us, because we were afraid.

The bear's paw prints were seen upon the top of the beaver dam. The crab-apple trees had long, deep scratches against their thick trunks. There were wide crushed paths through the raspberry bushes. We no longer collected the lichen, or dared to hunt for quartz crystals.

President Roosevelt's famous words "Let me assert my firm belief that the only thing we have to fear is fear itself" seem to fit here. Of course a bear can be dangerous, especially the bear of our ignorance and fear. To this day, thirty years after the hunter told us to be careful, I still cannot roam around my father's property with the same freedom I had when I filled my pockets with white stones.

Perhaps the bear sits in the secret place, licking the raspberry juice from his lips as he laughs and laughs at the fragile nature of us human beings, who do not dare to roar.

THROUGH THE
LOOKING
GLASS

I remember reading *The Lion, the Witch, and the Wardrobe,*
Through the Looking Glass, and the *Arabian Nights.* All these
books gave me the idea there were things hidden behind drab
cupboards, magical worlds could be discovered by stepping
into mirrors, and treasures could be mine if I could only pry
open the stone cliffs.

With this notion in mind when I was ten, the time when
boys ought to have notions, I was curious to know if there
was any treasure hidden behind my bedroom wall.

The attic had been converted into a bedroom sixty years
before I was born. The walls were made of a soft, fiberlike
material, built within the larger shell of the attic's sloped
ceiling.

At some point I realized that there was a hollow space between the false wall of my room and the side of the house.

I slid down the banister to the second floor, casually walked down the second flight of stairs, passed the living room, where my parents were reading, and into the basement. Somewhere among the broken picture frames and bits of wood I found what I was looking for: a thin saw.

By the time I returned to my bedroom, I felt like a spy, or a boy who had stolen a pig from the market. I pulled the saw out from under my shirt.

Trying not to make much noise, I poked a hole into the east wall, pressed the nose of the saw into the hole, and began slowly, slowly cutting out an eight-inch square.

With the last pull upon the saw, the cut piece of wall fell back and disappeared into the darkness. Did I hear a distant lion's roar? Did someone order me to paint the roses red? Perhaps there was a genie laughing?

I grabbed a flashlight, thrust it and my arm into the hole, and pressed my chin upon the edge of the cut wall.

The beam of light illuminated the hidden beams and the sloping roof line. I looked to the left and to the right inside the hole, and then I turned my head downward. There on the hidden floor sat . . . a fly swatter. No magic rabbits. No queens or kings with an invitation to join them for croquet or a coronation, just a fly swatter.

The scientific community of this country launched the Hubble telescope into space, beyond the interference of the earth's atmosphere. It has been reported in *The New York Times* that if we stood outside on a clear night we could see six thousand objects in the night sky. With the largest earthbound telescope we could see forty billion objects in the distant night. With this new telescope we will be able to see five to ten trillion objects. There is speculation that with this telescope we will eventually be able to see deeper into the past, detect the beginning of time perhaps, detect the extent of the universe, map out the structure of the galaxies, discover new phenomena.

God isn't hiding there. I suspect there are hidden hopes that a new discovery will be made: a more powerful "big bang" notion, the rubbing of a black hole with the sides of moving light, and, poof, the universe was created out of extraordinary explainable, mathematically sound projections and equations.

This technology is a wonderful thing. I applaud our curiosity, but let us be cautious about the reverence we are tempted to apply to it. This technology will not lead us to the yellow brick road of salvation. This new venture is no different from a boy peering into a dark hole with his flashlight. A scientist discovers more stars. A child discovers a fly swatter.

We can extend our physical vision by projecting mechanical objects into the darkness, but the natural world will not reveal the ultimate secrets. It is in the act of human faith that we can discover the beginning of time. It is in the embrace of the person standing beside us that we can calculate our true destiny. The frontier is in our spiritual selves, not in the night sky.

THE WIND
MACHINE

After I finished reading Fyodor Dostoyevsky's novel *The Brothers Karamazov*, it was difficult for me to know where I had been during those weeks I spent with this book. My children knew the name Karamazov, for they saw me reading as I sat on the living-room couch and they ran from room to room hooting and laughing and teasing each other.

This book. What can we say about a man, or about a doubt that is always pulling at one's heart? This is what the book was about . . . man and his doubts.

Yesterday I made Indian feather headbands and paper tomahawks for the children. They also asked me to make a teepee. Perhaps in the summer I'll make the teepee.

There is a mysterious pleasure in reading a book that

contains universal truths. "There is no virtue if there is no immortality." . . . "The secret of the times and seasons is in the wisdom of God." . . . "Love one another." . . . "Life is paradise, and we are all in paradise, but we refuse to see it. If we would, we should have heaven on earth the next day." . . . "Every one is really responsible to all men for all men and for everything." . . . "It's the great mystery of human life that old grief passes gradually into quiet tender joy."

Much of our struggle in life is trying to reconcile ourselves with the evidence of truth that is placed before us. Perhaps that is the first punishment after the fall of Adam and Eve. We are denied a comfort. We are denied a certitude until we return to the first act of love, the creation of men and women for the sake of life and joy and innocence . . . but that return takes time and suffering.

Before I read the last twenty pages of the novel, I gave Karen and Michael and David showers. They like it when I carry them one by one to their bedrooms wrapped in warm towels. They like to play "wind machine." The idea is to wave the towel quickly around their bodies as I make a loud whirring sound and they bounce upon their beds. They quickly dry as they laugh and laugh.

After their showers I read *The Tale of Mr. Jeremy Fisher* to Michael and a chapter of *The Dream Stealer* to David (a wonderful story by Gregory Maguire about Baba Yaga), and Karen read a Berenstain Bear book to all of us.

On the last pages of Dostoyevsky's novel, Alyosha says, "You must know that there is nothing higher and stronger and more wholesome and good for life in the future than some good memory, especially a memory of childhood, of home. People talk to you a great deal about your education, but some good, sacred memory, preserved from childhood, is perhaps the best education."

Perhaps my children will remember Jeremy Fisher's good luck, or Baba Yaga's power. Perhaps the two boys will remember the voice of their sister reading aloud to them in the middle of their childhood many years ago. I carried Michael to bed with his paper Indian feathers upon his head.

We must reconcile ourselves with these mysterious pleasures of truth that exist all around us. Such reconciliation means that we have simply to recognize that these mysteries do exist, and they exist for our joy and salvation.

I hope my children always remember the wind machine.